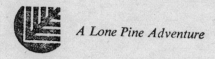
A Lone Pine Adventure

SEA WITCH COMES HOME

D1313505

This Armada book belongs to:

Susan Macrae

Sea Witch Comes Home

Malcolm Saville

Sea Witch Comes Home was first published in 1960 by
William Collins Sons & Co. Ltd., London and Glasgow.
First published in Armada in 1980 by
Fontana Paperbacks,
14 St. James's Place, London SW1A 1PS.

© Malcolm Saville 1960

Printed in Great Britain by
Love & Malcomson Ltd., Brighton Road,
Redhill, Surrey.

Contents

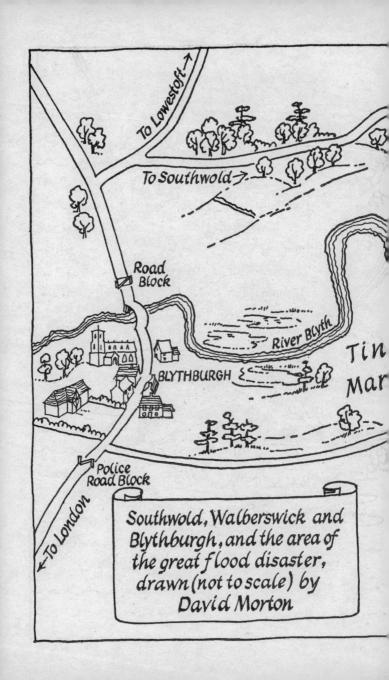

To Lowestoft →

To Southwold →

Road Block

River Blyth

Tin
Mar

BLYTHBURGH

Police
Road Block

← To London

Southwold, Walberswick and
Blythburgh, and the area of
the great flood disaster,
drawn (not to scale) by
David Morton

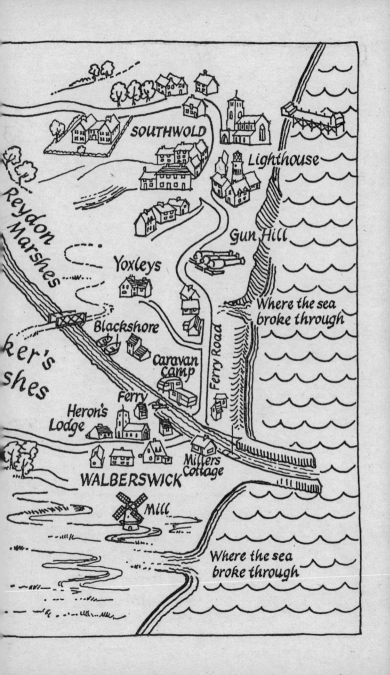

Foreword

NEARLY ALL my stories are set in country to which you can go yourself and most of the places described in these pages are real. The scene is a stretch of the east coast of England between Southwold and Orford which for centuries has been attacked by the sea and which is slowly crumbling away.

This is the country of sandy cliffs crowned with cornfields glowing with scarlet poppies, wide open skies which are an inspiration to artists, and magnificent parish churches built in the fifteenth century. The most remarkable of these is probably that at Blythburgh, which plays an important part in this story. You can go there yourself and see the broken brick floor at the west end which was smashed by Cromwell's soldiers when they stabled their horses in the church during the Civil War. On one of the church doors you can also see burns which are said to be the fingermarks of the Devil himself when he appeared in the church during a great thunderstorm in 1577!

This part of the coast is called Sole Bay, and when you are exploring it you may find all that is left of Dunwich which was once the greatest port in East Anglia, and remains of which can be seen at very low tide. Here, as the sandy cliffs break away, are sometimes found not only treasures left by those who lived in Dunwich hundreds of years ago, but the bones of those who were buried round the six churches of the ancient port.

Every mile of this unusual coast and the lovely country behind it is worth exploring. Southwold, with its white lighthouse towering over its streets of flint and red brick houses, is waiting for you to discover—and so is the harbour at the mouth of the river Blyth a mile away. Between the river and the town are the flat marshlands which were flooded when the sea broke through the defences not many years ago.

The marshes which Rose knew so well behind Walberswick across the river are real enough, too, as you will discover if you try to find your way to the old brick mill. Behind, and to the south of these marshes, are commons purple with heather which are the haunts of wild birds and of adders too.

The great storm in 1953, which did so much damage, attacked the east coast on the night of January 31st. The storm in this story reached Sole Bay early in September before the Mortons and Paul and Rose went back to school. Actually, the autumn equinox, when the tides are at their highest, comes a week or ten days later, so I have cheated a little for the sake of the plot!

So far as I know, there is no little coastal town in Holland called Zutten, nor a *Golden Eagle* hotel.

All the people in this story are imaginary, and there are no such houses as Heron's Lodge and Yoxleys and no inn called *Harbour Lights*.

I must also explain that this special edition is a little shorter than the original story which was first published in 1960, but the adventure, which I hope you will find exciting, has not been altered.

M. S.

THE PEOPLE IN THE STORY

SIMON DONALD	An international picture dealer.
JUAN ANDREA	Donald's best customer.
RICHARD CHANNING	Widower living at Heron's Lodge, Walberswick and father of

PAUL CHANNING	Age seventeen, and his sister
ROSE CHANNING	Age twelve.
WILLIAM MILLER	Fisherman friend of the Channings, and his wife
MARY MILLER	
EMMA HOLMES	Housekeeper at Yoxleys.
JAMES WILSON	A reporter on the London *Clarion*.
GEORGE SUMMERS	A detective from Scotland Yard.

There are also some accomplices of Donald's and three of the Lone Piners and their parents.

THE LONE PINE CLUB

The boys and girls known as the Lone Piners have had twelve previous adventures, and if you have read any of them you will know that they are so called because they founded a secret society known as the Lone Pine Club at a lonely house called Witchend in the heart of the Shropshire hills.

The rules of the Club are still hidden under the solitary pine tree in their first secret camp. They are very simple and are set out in full in *Mystery at Witchend*, which is the first Lone Pine story. All the members signed the oath in his or her own blood—*Every member of the Lone Pine Club swears to keep the rules and to be true to each other whatever happens always*.

There are nine members and it is rare for them all to appear in one story. In this one there are only three— DAVID MORTON, age sixteen, was elected captain of the Club when it was founded. He lives in London. Not particularly clever but above the average at work and games. Not much of a talker. Thoroughly dependable and a good leader.

RICHARD ("DICKIE") MORTON and his sister MARY are ten-year-old twins. Although the youngest members of the Club and often extremely irritating to the others, they have proved their worth in all the Lone Piners' adventures. Alike in looks and speech, they have a maddening trick of pretending to be younger than they are, and when in action together they annoy most grown-ups. They get their own way too often, but with all their faults they are warm-hearted, loyal and courageous and will tackle anything to justify themselves to the other members of the Club. Their constant companion is a little black Scottie named Macbeth by their father because as a puppy he "murdered sleep."

1. The "Golden Eagle"

ONE SUNNY AFTERNOON half-way through August a tall, handsome, well-dressed man was sitting at the window on the first floor of a hotel called the *Golden Eagle* in the small Dutch port of Zutten. The window, which was open because the day was warm, looked out upon the wharf and the harbour basin, and there was just enough breeze from the sea to disperse the fragrant blue smoke from the man's cigar.

It was easy to see that he was neither Dutch nor British. His suit looked too expensive, a diamond flashed from the ring on his finger, and although his dark hair was flecked with grey his complexion was swarthy. Two days ago, on arrival, he had signed the hotel register as Juan Andrea and given his nationality as a small country in South America.

Now he was waiting for a visitor. He looked at his watch, got up and shrugged his shoulders and then paced up and down the only private sitting-room in the hotel.

There was no reason to believe that the plane from London would be late at Rotterdam, and the visitor he was expecting should soon be there. He had arranged for a fast car to bring him to Zutten, to wait and to return.

Andrea went back to the window in time to see a sleek black car draw up outside the hotel. He could not see his visitor, about whom he was very curious, but almost by the time he had moved a box of cigars from the mantelpiece to the table by his chair there was a knock on the door.

He called "Come in", and walked across to greet his guest.

For a moment the two men studied each other carefully, and then Andrea held out his hand.

"Mr Simon Donald? Good afternoon. I hope you have had a pleasant journey. I appreciate a visit at such short notice. Come and sit down by the window . . . Cigar? May

13

I offer you other refreshment?"

Donald shook his head.

"Nothing, thank you, Mr Andrea. Shall we get down to business? I have to be back in London this evening."

Andrea raised his eyebrows in surprise. Nobody would have mistaken his visitor for anybody but an Englishman for his tweed suit, silk tie, and dark tan shoes were typical. He was short and slim, his voice was quiet, his little grey moustache neatly trimmed, and although his face and expression were unremarkable his eyes, behind his rimless glasses, were a cold ice-blue. But for those eyes it is unlikely that anyone would have looked at him twice.

Andrea bowed slightly and sat down. His English was nearly faultless and only occasionally did his accent suggest that it was not his native language.

"Very well, Mr Donald. We will waste no more time. Your reputation as a dealer in works of art has been known to me for many years. Indeed, whenever there is talk of pictures in the sale rooms of Europe and America the name of Simon Donald is respected. I wrote to you because I believe you are the greatest living expert on British painting and I have an important commission for you."

"Thank you, Mr Andrea. Or should I say Señor Andrea?"

"Just Andrea will do, Mr Donald. No doubt you have been wondering why I asked you to meet me here, in this small town, rather than in London?"

"I have my own ideas, Mr Andrea. I am a business man and you have paid me well to come here. I understand you are interested in the landscape paintings of John Jackson? May I ask why? I have none to sell you."

"I am interested because I have a very wealthy client in my country who intends to make a collection of this artist's work. I will, you see, do what you call place my cards on the table. I know a little about art and I am sure that Jackson's work—I have not seen more than four of his pictures—is going to be extremely valuable before long. Do you agree?"

"I do not believe that you have asked me to come here to give you my advice, Mr Andrea. You have not even offered to pay me for advice, but I am prepared to say that, like you, I have a great respect for this artist's work and believe his early death to be a tragedy. But how can I help you? Jackson, who, so far as we know, was not married, left no record of his work. Six of his paintings are in public Art Galleries in my country and perhaps there are twenty or so in private collections. I know where eight of these are, but I do not believe that any of the owners wish to sell. I can try for you, of course, but you and your client are not alone in your faith in John Jackson. Occasionally, of course, an owner may wish to sell, and occasionally no doubt a J.J. painting will turn up in a junk shop in East Anglia."

"East Anglia? What is that? I do not know those words."

"The part of my country nearest to this Dutch town. The East Coast, we sometimes call it. My guess would be that the owner of every second-hand shop in Britain has, during the last few weeks, looked very carefully through his stock for a J.J.. You are not the only customer for his pictures, Mr Andrea, and I do not see what I can do to help you. Many people are aware that Jackson's pictures are rapidly increasing in value."

"Tell me more about this remarkable young man and his work, if you please, Mr Donald. Are not all his canvasses rather small?"

"We think so. I have never heard of a big picture. Jackson was born and lived for many years in a small town called Southwold on our east coast. It is an attractive place, always much favoured by artists, and the country round, although flat, has a certain charm. But the skies and the light are magnificent, and all Jackson's work shows how much he was impressed by these qualities. Just over a year ago some people in Southwold arranged a show of this artist's work and borrowed some of the pictures that are privately owned. This started the fashion for J.J. pictures, although there is no doubt of their quality . . . All I can do is to see if I can find one or two of them for you, but I warn you that you may not like the price and they may take a long time to get."

Andrea leaned forward and took another cigar.

"I would not have asked you to come here to meet me, sir, if this had not been a matter of very considerable importance," he said slowly and carefully. "Indeed you would not be here if I had not proved to you how important I and my client believe this matter to be. Shall we say that as many John Jackson pictures as possible are wanted for investment? It would be wrong of me not to tell you now that they are required quickly. I and my friends have plenty of money to invest but we cannot wait too long. Call it a whim if you will, but we are prepared to pay well for what we want. And we want genuine John Jackson pictures and have reason to believe that you can get them for us."

The two men stared at each other in silence.

"I see," Donald said at last. "What sort of sum are you prepared to invest in each picture?"

Andrea, with a gold pencil, wrote a figure on the edge of *The Times* which was on the table between them.

"I always read your English newspapers when I can," he said as he passed it over. "*The Times* of the day arrives here each morning."

Donald glanced at the pencilled figure and if he was surprised he did not show it.

"For quick delivery there might be an even larger investment," Andrea murmured as he tore the marked strip from the paper and burned it in the ash-tray. "I do not want to be in Europe too long and it is not convenient for me to come to England. I shall stay here until I hear from you, if you are prepared to do business. Are you?"

Donald stood up and looked out at the little ships in the harbour basin.

"I am a business man," he said quietly. "I think it will be possible for me to please you and your clients, and this place is really very convenient for delivery. I must make it clear, Mr Andrea, that I am not likely to repeat this trip. I am more comfortable in my own country."

Again the two men regarded each other in silence. At last, "How shall I know when to expect your messenger, my friend? And how shall I recognize him—or her?"

Donald picked up *The Times*.

"Within the next few days," he promised, "I will write to you here explaining that on the day you read in the Personal column of *The Times* a code message which I shall explain to you in the letter, you can expect my messenger within twenty-four hours. Please remember, however, that I do not care to trust valuable pictures to air travel. My messenger will be unobtrusive and trustworthy and will arrive by sea—right here, Mr Andrea, on your doorstep. If we cannot deliver two or more pictures at a time we will deliver one as soon as possible as a sign of good faith. As you know, sir, the expenses of sending out a number of experienced picture dealers more or less at the same time is very heavy. Have you any suggestions?"

Andrea nodded and walked into his bedroom and closed the door while Donald, as unruffled as when he had arrived, continued to gaze out of the window with his cold blue eyes. He did not even turn round until Andrea came back.

"Travelling expenses, my dear sir. Perhaps you would care to check the amount and sign this receipt."

Donald took the Bank of England notes, counted them, put them in his pocket, and then read what was written on a sheet of *Golden Eagle* notepaper. After a moment's thought he scribbled his signature on it and passed it back.

"Good afternoon, Mr Andrea," he said politely, as he picked up his hat and pretended not to see his host's outstretched hand. "My car is waiting and I shall return at once to the airport. When you have heard from me in a few days, you will watch *The Times* very carefully. Do not, I beg, write to me in London more than is necessary and be certain not to telephone me unless there is an emergency—such as a change of address on your part."

He did not look back as he left the room, nor did he look up before getting into his car and driving off.

Andrea stood for a while tapping his teeth with his gold pencil. He looked worried as he shrugged his shoulders and muttered, "These English! They are like the cold fish. But he is surely the best man and I think he understood me."

2. London

Somewhere between the shabby districts of north London known as Islington and Finsbury Park is a quiet corner called Brownlow Square. All the houses here are tall and narrow with steps leading down to dark basements, but many of them have been brightened up with fresh paint and coloured front doors. The people who live in Brownlow Square know that it is not yet smart nor fashionable, but it is quiet and within easy reach of the centre of London, and close to shops and an underground station.

The Morton family live at Number Seven, which has a scarlet front door—like a fire station, Dickie says—and we meet them at half past eight on a September morning.

Mr Morton liked his breakfast in peace, so he began his meal in the school holidays before David and the twins. On this particular morning David arrived just as his father got up.

"'Morning. Hope I'm not too late. Smells like kippers this morning. Talk to me while I have mine, Mum. I think the twins are murdering each other in the bathroom."

Mrs Morton went out into the hall to say "Good-bye" to her husband while David settled down to cornflakes. He was barely average height for sixteen and good-looking in a plain sort of way. Thick, fairish to brown hair, wide humorous mouth and steady grey eyes. Physically he was strong, with the well-developed shoulders of a cricketer.

As his mother came back with his kipper and poured out his tea and another cup for herself, the ceiling shook as something heavy fell on the floor of the room above. Macbeth, the family's black Scottie, sat up and put his head on one side. Then, as the twins came bounding downstairs, he stood up and wagged his tail in greeting.

The Morton twins, Richard and Mary, were ten. They were astonishingly alike in feature, voice, and character and there really was great sympathy between them.

"We're sorry," Mary began. "Very sorry, but we were in such a hurry trying not to be late for breakfast that we've had a bit of an accident upstairs, Mum."

"If you heard a little sort of tap on the floor," Dickie went on as he scowled at David, "that was the accident. Nobody came, but I could easily be dead. We happened to be in David's room looking for something when Mary happened jus' to brush against me in passing an' fell over a chair that David had selfishly left in the middle of the room."

"And it's no use scowling like that, David," Mary said quickly. "It *is* careless to leave furniture where people can fall over it. Dangerous too."

Dickie sat down next to his brother. "I might as well tell you, Mum, that the back of the chair is a bit cracked. It wouldn't be safe to lean back in if you know what I mean . . . Cornflakes, please."

Mrs Morton tried to look severe.

"Is David's chair *really* broken, Richard?"

"If he has broken it, he'll have to spend his pocket money to mend it," David said grimly. "Time those children went back to school. Pity I'm not allowed to discipline them."

Mary got off her chair and gave her mother a hug. "The chair's only a bit cracked, Mummy, and we *are* sorry . . . You stay there and I'll get the kippers, and I think the post has just come."

She came back with a plate in each hand and some letters between her teeth. When the former were safely on the table she sorted through the post and passed all but one envelope to her mother.

"Oh! Oh, twin! Look at that. A lovely letter for our big brother. Look, Dickie. A strange writing and we can't read the postmark except that it's Norfolk or Suffolk. Mummy! David has got a girl-friend we don't know about——"

Then she saw the fierce expression on her brother's face and passed the letter over quickly without another word.

David looked at the handwriting in puzzled surprise and then read the letter in silence. When he had finished, he folded it up, stuffed it in his pocket and rather absent-mindedly spread some marmalade on his toast.

"Bad news, David?" his mother asked.

"No, Mum. Not bad. Just surprising. I'm puzzled about it. I'll tell you some time."

"Why not now?" Dickie suggested.

David shook his head while Mrs Morton said quietly, "That will do, twins. You've talked enough for one meal. What are you going to do this morning?"

The twins saw David's worried face and took the hint.

"We are going to Hampstead Heath," Mary said. "Soon and quickly. With Mackie. We shall be back for lunch."

Half an hour later when the twins had gone, David, who was helping his mother in the kitchen, said,

"I'd like to tell you about that letter, Mum. It's from Paul Channing at Walberswick."

"Paul Channing? Your friend at school? You went to stay there last Easter with the twins, didn't you? And he came here with his sister for a week-end? Of course I remember them. Why is he writing to you?"

"I'm not sure. He wants me to meet him at Liverpool Street station at a quarter to twelve this morning, and it all sounds rather mysterious and worrying. I don't know why he won't come here. He sounds as if he's in trouble and needs help, but I can't make him out. Paul is an excitable sort of bloke and it's an odd sort of home. Something important must have happened to make him write like this."

Mrs Morton passed David a drying-up cloth.

"Get busy, David, and tell me more about the Channings. There isn't a mother, is there?"

"No. She's dead but I don't know when. Paul never speaks of her and neither does young Rose. Paul is six months older than me. Rose is twelve. Nice kid. Pony tail and big eyes. Mr Channing is good fun, but he wasn't often at home. He's got a boat and he's keen on shooting, too. Then there is Aunt Jane who is a sort of housekeeper."

"What does Mr Channing do besides sailing and shooting?"

"I don't really know. I've never asked Paul and I wouldn't anyway. We all liked him and he was very good company. Nice-looking chap and very strong. Can't imagine him doing an ordinary sort of job, somehow . . . I'll have to go now, Mum, and I don't suppose I'll be back to lunch. If he'll come I'll bring him up here, but I'll telephone first . . . Why can't he say straight out what he wants?"

"I'm sure you'll be able to help him, David. Bring him back here for the night if he'll come."

And so David changed and hurried out.

Not long afterwards he was settled on the front seat in the bus and took Paul's letter from his pocket and read it again.

> *Heron's Lodge,*
> *Walberswick,*
> *Suffolk.*
>
> *Dear David,*
> *Sorry to be dramatic but this is urgent and important. I want to see you at once and I can't explain why in this letter. I'm coming to London specially tomorrow arriving Liverpool Street* 11.45. *Please meet me there and take me where we can talk privately and you've got to understand that I don't want to come to Brownlow Square. I've got to get back here as soon as I can. No more now except that I'm very fussed about something and you can help me.*
> *Paul.*
> *If you're not at L. St. I shall telephone Brownlow Square but I don't want to do that. I want to talk to you in person.*

Paul Channing was not one of David's closest friends, although he had known him for three years and liked him as opposites often do like each other. He was six months older, much better looking and much more temperamental and moody.

David sighed as he looked out the window. Where could he take Paul for a quiet talk, and what dark secret was he going to hear? The bus crawled. The traffic lights were always red. Nobody seemed to care when they got to Liverpool Street, and even David was beginning to worry when at last they stopped outside the station at five minutes to twelve.

David pushed through the crowds and was hot and rather bad-tempered when he reached the arrival platform. A porter found time to tell him that the Norwich train had been in for ten minutes. When he reached the platform there was no sign of Paul, and David realized that it was typical of his friend not to say *where* he expected to be met. David considered and then had a brainwave. The telephone kiosks, of course! He was right. Eight people were waiting in various stages of impatience outside the nearest kiosks and Paul, with the usual lock of dark hair drooping over his forehead, was fidgeting in the queue.

David touched him on the shoulder.

"Sorry I'm late, Paul. It was the bus. London traffic hardly moves these days. What's the trouble?"

Paul grabbed his arm and pulled him away from the other waiting people.

"So you've turned up after all, have you? I don't ask much of my friends and I should have thought it was simple enough for you to get here on time."

"Oh, shut up!" David said. "You're making a fool of yourself and you're lucky I'm here. What's all the mystery and why couldn't you come to Brownlow Square? You know that you can come there when you like."

With a quick change of mood Paul flashed him a smile.

"Sorry! Sorry! O.K., David. I'll tell you all about it. Thank you for coming. Where shall we go?"

Then David remembered the Embankment Gardens where there was a café with chairs and tables on a paved terrace.

Paul agreed to this suggestion and after a short bus ride they reached the Gardens.

The two boys queued for coffee and sandwiches and then were lucky to find a vacant table.

"You've come a long way to talk, Paul," David said as he sat down. "What's the trouble? You can trust me."

Paul looked up at the seagulls sailing so effortlessly overhead, and when he turned to look at David his eyes were troubled.

"It's difficult to say but I've got to do it," he began. "You've been to stay with us at Heron's Lodge and I suppose you realized that it's not the same at home for Rose and me as it is for you at Brownlow Square."

"You mean because you haven't got a mother?" David prompted.

"That's got something to do with it, of course. I can remember Mother but Rose can't . . . Truth is that I'm worried about Father, David. He's disappeared and hasn't told us where he's gone or when he will be back!"

"But he often goes away, doesn't he? He went off sailing or fishing for three days last time we were staying with you."

"I know that, David. Trouble is that it's different this time because he hasn't told us anything. And Aunt Jane is on holiday for a month and that doesn't make things any easier. He had a letter from London about a week ago and came up here by car directly after breakfast. At least he *said* he'd been to London and next day he was excited and rather peculiar, and although Rose can usually get anything out of him, he wouldn't tell us about his visit except to hint that everything was going to be much better for us soon."

"Much better for you, Paul? What did he mean? Things aren't too bad at home, are they?"

"I s'pose not. It's difficult to say, but Rose doesn't seem to realize that sometimes Father seems to have plenty of money and other times he's worried and says we can't afford new clothes and that we'll have to sell *Sea Witch*. Day before yesterday I'd been to Southwold with Rose, and when we came back he'd gone and we haven't seen him since. He left a note—I haven't brought it—but he told us not to worry, that he didn't know when he would be back, but he wouldn't be away for long and why didn't we ask you and the twins to come up for a week. He didn't say anything about Aunt Jane– I expect he'd forgotten that she was away."

"But why are you so worried, Paul? You've said he often goes away. Surely that's all he's done now?"

"He's always told us before where he'll be and when he'll be back. I know that when we're at school he's away a lot too, but I'm sure that this time it's different and I'd give anything to know where he is."

He paused and looked down at his fingers resting on the iron table. Then,

"There's another thing, and I wouldn't say this to any-body but you. I just feel that there was something not quite right about that sudden trip to London and his excitement when he came back. It was almost as if he'd suddenly got a lot of money. He left ten pounds for us in the letter, by the way, but that won't last long when you arrive tomorrow."

David looked at him curiously.

"But why are you worrying specially? And why do you want us to come so quickly? Has something happened that you haven't told me?"

"It's because nothing else has happened that I'm worried. He *always* tells us where he's going. I can't put it properly into words, David, but I've got a fear that his going off selfishly like this and leaving us without any real news has got something to do with money . . . Now do you see why I'm so anxious?"

David still could not understand why Paul was so upset, but he did not know much about Mr Channing. He remembered him as a handsome, tanned, middle-aged man dressed in old tweeds and nearly always talking about sport. He had laughed a lot, showing very white teeth under a neat moustache, and was always teasing the twins. But, come to think of it, he had behaved like a man who was on holiday in his own home.

"With money, Paul? What do you mean? What does your father do? Has he got a job?"

Paul shook his head.

"Not as far as I know. Sometimes I've thought we must be quite well off. Other times, as I said just now, he gets worried and says he doesn't know how much longer I shall be at school. And when we're away I just don't know what he does or where he goes . . . Truth is, David, I feel something is very wrong. I can't talk to Rose about it because she'll never hear a word against Father and anyway she's only twelve and why should I worry her? You told me once that you and those friends of yours up in Shropshire and those cousins from Rye have had more than one adventure together. Come up to Walberswick tomorrow and stand by with me. That's what I want. We haven't got many friends up there. I've made up my mind I'm going to find Father. Will you help me, David? Bring the twins as company for Rose. I couldn't bring her today—couldn't afford two fares —but she knows I'm asking you to come tomorrow."

"Where is she then? Alone in Heron's Lodge?"

"She never minds being alone, but she'll be with William and Mary."

"William and Mary?"

"Don't you remember them? We always call the Millers William and Mary. He's a fisherman and his cottage is down by the river. Will you come, David? You'll have to ask your parents, I know, but you can tell them that Father has had to go off for a few days, that Aunt Jane is on holiday and that we want your company and your help. That's all true. Have you had your holiday yet? Been away I mean?"

David shook his head.

"All the better then. You need sea air! We'll give you a good holiday. Explain to your mother, David, and say I'm sorry I couldn't come up to see her. Now I must go back to Liverpool Street. There's a slow train that takes hours but I must catch it. Telephone me tonight please—Walberswick 4490."

"O.K., Paul. I'm sure we'll be able to come. What time shall I phone?"

"After nine. Better make it ten. Whatever else we do, we'll be back home by then. I'll be waiting for you by the phone. You come to Halesworth station tomorrow and take the bus to Walberswick. There's a ten-thirty from London."

*   *   *

At home in Brownlow Square David told his mother everything, except Paul's odd suggestion that his father's sudden absence was something to do with money. He admitted that Paul was worried and wanted help, and added that he would very much like to go.

Mrs Morton seemed to think it a good idea, so did Dickie and Mary, and Mr Morton agreed when he came home, so that was all very satisfactory.

There was a lot of confusion and argument throughout the evening over the twins' packing and they were not in bed until ten. Mr and Mrs Morton went up early, so David was alone downstairs with the telephone a few minutes after the time arranged.

He had Walberswick 4490 written down and he heard the ringing tone about a minute after asking for the number.

There was no reply.

He got the exchange again, rechecked the number, heard it repeated and a man's voice say, "I'm ringing them now, London."

There was still no reply, and feeling suddenly apprehensive David looked at the clock and saw that the time was twenty minutes past ten.

He put down the receiver, waited a long fifteen minutes and tried again.

He could hear the *Brrr-Brrr-Brrr* of the ringing tone and that was all.

He rang again at 10.50 and again at 11 p.m.

There was no reply.

In spite of his promise Paul was not at Heron's Lodge, and where was Rose?

3. The Red Mill

WE FIRST MEET Rose Channing at breakfast at Heron's Lodge just before Paul set off for London to meet David. Although not as excitable as her brother, she had an eager, gay personality which showed itself most obviously when she was in the company of those she liked. She gave her father far more love than he gave in return, only tolerated her aunt, and was prepared to put up with Paul when he did not tease her or interfere when she wanted to go off by herself on the marshes and commons of Suffolk. Rose was not easy to know but her affection was worth winning.

When Paul came clattering downstairs for his breakfast, Rose, in jeans and a red checked shirt, was at the cooker looking with loathing at the cold fat in the frying-pan.

"Buck up, Rose. I'm in a hurry. Is it bacon?"

"No. There isn't any. We forgot to buy it yesterday, but there's toast and marmalade and a tin of sardines. I was just wondering whether we could fry the sardines in this mess of fat. People *do* have hot, cooked sardines, don't they? And anyway if you want an early breakfast, there's no reason why you shouldn't come down earlier to get it for yourself."

Paul scowled and then decided not to squabble.

"All right, Rosie. Cold sardines are a good idea."

When he began his meal, Rose sat at the other end of the kitchen table and rested her chin on her hands.

"I'll eat when you've gone, Paul. I've got all day to do nothing in. I'd like to have David and the twins here to-morrow, but why don't you tell me why you've got into such a panic about Daddy? Why have you *got* to go to London? You're worried about something and you won't tell me. I know it's a nuisance that Aunt Jane has gone off but we've been alone before. Why have you got to *speak* to David about them coming here? I don't think you should to tell the Mortons that we don't know where Daddy is. That's our business. I expect we shall hear from him today. There'll be a letter, Paul. Or he'll telephone. I know he will. You'll be sorry that you're not here. Why are you going to meet David today?"

Paul mumbled because his mouth was full.

"I want to make sure that they'll come tomorrow. Father has no right to go off and leave us alone here without telling us where he's going and what he's doing. You may not have noticed, Rose, but he was different after going to London the other day. He's got some secret and if the Mortons are here with us it will help us not to worry. Anyway I've got to explain to David before they come about him going off like this. Now stop fussing and have your breakfast. What are you going to do all day?"

Rose helped herself to toast and marmalade.

"Don't tell me to stop fussing. You're the fussy one with your silly ideas about Daddy. Don't say too much to the Mortons and make us both look silly. Me? I'll go and see William and Mary and have my dinner with them. You'll be on the last bus, I suppose? If I'm not here when you come I'll leave you a note. You'd better go now. I'll see you off."

"Come on then," he said as he got up from the table. "Sorry to leave all this mess to you. We'll have a grand clear-up tonight or tomorrow before they come."

Heron's Lodge stood fifty yards back from Walberswick's only street. It was the third house on the left as you entered the village from Blythburgh, which was indeed the only way by which anything on wheels could get to them. It was an odd-looking house with a wooden veranda along the front of it—a veranda on which the Channings kept their rubber boots, fishing tackle and all sorts of odds and ends. The kitchen and scullery were at the back, and along two-thirds of the front, facing the road, was the exciting, untidy living-room lined with books and old prints of birds and ships at sea and the great brick fireplace. Upstairs, where the floors creaked and groaned in the gales that screamed over the east coast when the nights were long, were five bedrooms, and outside, fixed to the great central chimney, was a silvered weathervane in the shape of a heron.

Rose grabbed an apple and ran down the veranda steps after Paul, who was hurrying to the gate with still five minutes to spare. It was a lovely morning—fresh and keen with a northerly wind bringing the murmur of the sea and smell of salt and mud from the river just over a quarter of a mile away—and the sun was already warm.

There were not many people about yet. All through the summer Walberswick was packed with families on holiday, for the sandy beach was ideal for young children and there was sailing and fishing and riding for those who were older. Just beyond the *Royal Oak* from where the bus started, the road turned sharply to the left, wandered over a small green and past some shops to the mouth of the river Blyth and the harbour. And here it stopped. There was no bridge across to Southwold.

"Have a good time, Paul," Rose said as the bus arrived. "My love to those twins. It'll be fun if they come tomorrow. I'll be O.K. with William and Mary."

She waved good-bye to her brother and ran back to Heron's Lodge where she fetched a pair of binoculars from the sitting-room, locked up the house and set out for the marshes.

There were two ways of getting to the old red brick water mill which, for as long as she could remember, had been one of her most secret and exciting places. Both ways were difficult because, although the mill in the middle of the flat marsh could be seen from a long way off, there was no track which went straight to it. The marsh was drained by dykes which seemed to wander without reason between steep banks fringed with bulrushes, and the only tracks were on a few of the causeways on the top of these banks.

The quickest way was along the track below the great bank of sand and shingle which kept the sea from flooding the marshes. For ten minutes Rose walked south along the top of the dunes with the beach and the sea on her left. Ahead of her the gentle bow of Sole Bay curved round to the crumbling cliffs of the forgotten port of Dunwich. On her right, the wind was rustling the rushes fringing the dykes, and nearly half a mile away she saw the familiar shape of the old mill standing on a little green island in the midst of the dykes. Soon she scrambled down the bank on to the path thick with mauve sea-asters, and then crossed a narrow foot-bridge over a wide ditch and stepped up to the track along the top of a causeway. Within a few minutes she was again aware of the loneliness and solitude of the marsh. As she walked forward, there was no sound but the sighing of the wind in the rushes and the sudden raucous cry of a bird. Rose stood still and raised the binoculars to her eyes. The cry was that of a great crested grebe, and she knew that a pair had nested not far from the old mill from which she had often watched them.

She walked on to the mill and then realized that she had forgotten the key to the rusty padlock which her father had given her two years ago. There were no sweeps now on the mill which had been built in its unusual position to pump water from a wide ditch up to the higher level of a much bigger dyke which eventually found its way into the river. Neither Rose nor Paul were interested in the machinery which had once been set in motion by the whirling sweeps, but the mill made a splendid hiding-place and it was not too difficult to clamber up to a wooden platform under the domed roof. From this vantage point they could see through peepholes where they had dragged some bricks away, out to sea in one direction, and over the roofs of Walberswick to Southwold and its white lighthouse away to the north.

Rose idly tried the padlock but it was fast, so she sat for a few minutes with her back against the warm brickwork and thought about her father.

She knew that Paul was more worried about his absence than he cared to admit. She was worried too, but realized with horror that Paul was actually suspicious of him and did not want her to know this.

Suddenly she decided that there was little sense in brooding here alone. Mary Miller would be pleased to see her, and she knew that she could spend the day in her cottage. It was sometimes awkward when William or Mary asked her about her father but she thought she could manage them.

She walked back the longer, inland way to the village, along narrow tracks by the dykes shoulder-high in reeds. And she walked unsuspecting straight into the beginning of her greatest adventure.

The Millers' cottage was but fifty yards from the bank of the river and within hailing distance of the black wooden hut where old Adam, the ferryman, sat waiting for his customers. The cottage was built of Suffolk flint with a red-tiled roof and, with its patch of garden, was surrounded by a whitewashed wall. The road finished almost at the front gate, and when Rose arrived there she was surprised to see a low, green sports car outside.

Rose heard the murmur of voices from inside the cottage and then saw a stranger, standing just inside the door. He was a very presentable young man of middle height, lean and tough-looking, with untidy hair and wearing a shabby sports jacket with a folded newspaper sticking out of the pocket. He turned at the sound of her step and smiled.

"You've got a visitor, Mrs Miller. Hope I'm not in the way but I've still got plenty of questions to ask you."

"Hello, Mary," said Rose, "I've come to dinner if you'll have me."

Mary Miller had been married to her William for twenty years but had no children. Like her husband, she was Suffolk born and bred. Mr Channing had been at Heron's Lodge when she came to the cottage at Walberswick as a bride from Southwold, so she remembered Paul and Rose's mother and had seen the two children growing up. Her husband knew Mr Channing better than she did but there was a great bond between Rose and herself.

She stepped forward with a welcoming smile. "Hello,

love. Come along in and listen to this young man's gossip. You may have heard your father talk of an artist chap called John Jackson who was born in Southwold and lived around here for years. What did you say your name was? You'd better meet Rose Channing."

"I'm James Wilson. Hello, Rose."

He shook hands and then went on,

"If you're not both too busy, I suggest we sit out in the sunshine on your wall. I won't keep you long, Mrs Miller, but I was told at the post office that you've lived in the district all your life. I want to find out something about this artist Jackson and I'll tell you why."

Mr Wilson took them both firmly by the arm and led them outside.

"Now listen, ladies, and I will come clean. I am not what I seem. I am a reporter on the staff of the London *Clarion*, and I will show you why I want to find out something about John Jackson, an artist who lived round here and who, before he died about ten years ago, painted many pictures of this part of the country . . . See here."

At this he took a folded paper from his pocket, opened it and stabbed it with his finger at a headline—THREE J.J. PICTURES STOLEN THIS WEEK. Above the big type was a reproduction of a landscape.

When she saw the latter Rose squeaked with excitement.

"But that's a picture of my mill! I've just come from there. Look, Mary! It's our mill, but when the artist painted it the sweeps were on it."

"Sure, Rose?" Wilson asked sharply. "This is one of Jackson's most famous pictures and is known as the Red Mill. It was stolen from a judge's house in Dulwich in south-east London just a week ago."

"Of course I'm sure. I could easily take you to the mill. But why does it matter?"

"It matters a lot, Rose. I want a story for my paper about John Jackson who was born and lived in Southwold and who painted so many Suffolk landscapes. There are some interesting features about his work which is now becoming much more than a fashion—it is a craze both here and in America, and collectors are paying very big prices for J.J. paintings . . . No. Don't go away, Mrs Miller. You are one of the people who might remember Jackson and I want to know everything that anybody round here knows about him."

Mrs Miller leaned against the wall, put an arm round Rose's shoulders and frowned as she struggled to remember.

"There'll be some in Southwold 'll remember him sure enough. Odd chap he was with a red beard and old clothes, but there's often artists in Southwold and we're used to seeing them about. This Jackson lived by himself at the top of the town. I can't remember that he was married, poor chap. I don't reckon anybody thought much of him, and now that he's dead his pictures are worth a lot o' money, you say? Ah, well, that's life I suppose!"

"It's a jolly unfair life anyway," Rose said indignantly. "And why are people stealing his pictures now, Mr Wilson? And how do they know who to steal them from?"

"That's a good question, Rose. Somebody very clever knows where they are, and I think that's because two years ago there was an exhibition of his pictures in Southwold and many were bought then. Anyway three have been stolen in a week. The J.J. pictures, which were always landscapes, are quite small so they'd be easy to hide without their frames. The police are after this thief, and I want to be about when he's caught because there's a big story here. Perhaps your parents will remember something about John Jackson, Rose?"

Rose coloured and looked away.

"I've never heard my father say anything about him, but he's away just now. If we hear anything, though, we'll tell you, won't we, Mary?"

"I suppose so, love, although the chap's dead and I think he's best left alone. Now I must put the dinner on, so I'll say 'Good morning', Mr Wilson."

Wilson smiled and gave her a card with his name and the London telephone number printed on it.

"I'll be about," he said. "I'll be seeing you, I'm sure, and if you remember anything or can find out more about John Jackson or his pictures, just let me know. Telephone London and ask for me. The paper will pay for a good story."

They watched the car roar off towards the village and then ran back to the cottage.

"A nice young man," Mrs Miller observed as she put a large shepherd's pie into the oven. "A busy young man though. Nosey, too. Can't think why the newspapers don't mind their own business. Where's your father, love? And where's Paul?"

"Daddy's away again, Mary. Paul has gone to London to ask some friends to come and stay with us. I'll bring them to see you. David is a bit younger than Paul and the twins are ten. P'raps you saw them when they came last year, though? They've got a little black Scottie dog called Macbeth."

Mary Miller gave the girl a very straight look.

"And so Paul has had to go to London to ask these friends? You're welcome to be here, dearie, as long as you like . . . And when's your Dad coming back, Rose? William was asking about him this very morning. Has he gone off in *Sea Witch*?"

"We're not sure, Mary. We don't know where Daddy is or when he'll be back. He left us a note telling us not to worry and I'm not going to. He'll come back as soon as he can and that will be when he's ready. It was his idea that we should have some friends, and so I hope the Mortons will come. And if anybody asks *you*, Mary, if you know where my father is you jolly well tell them to mind their own business. Please do that."

"Yes, love, I'll do that," Mrs Miller smiled and did not mention Mr Channing again.

After dinner Rose went across on the ferry to Southwold and spent the afternoon there. She loved the grassy greens fringed with houses and the big common between the town and the river. She liked the shops, too, and bought Mary a pot plant.

William was at home when Rose returned to Walberswick, and she was very pleased to see him. William was a man of few words, but she sensed at once that Mary and he had been talking about her father and about Paul going off to London without her.

It was a calm, lovely evening and when they had finished supper Rose went out and sat on the river bank. The brown and muddy tide was swirling up the estuary over which the gulls were crying, and farther up the river she could see the little boats of the sailing club busy twisting and turning in the stream as they tried to catch the breeze.

The bus from Halesworth was due at ten minutes past eight. It connected with the train from Ipswich and Paul would be on it. At eight, Rose said "Good-bye" to William and Mary, promised to come and see them tomorrow and then walked up to the *Royal Oak*.

At twenty past eight she was still waiting for the bus, and by half past she began to worry. *Why couldn't the bus come?*

Then she heard it and felt a fool for beginning to panic.

Four women and three young men got off. And that was all. No Paul.

"What's happened?" she said to the conductor. "Why are you late? Have you seen my brother? He was on the London train."

"No London train, miss. Sorry but we couldn't wait at Halesworth no longer. They say there's a long delay for all trains north from Ipswich."

"But how will he get home? Are you going back to Halesworth to fetch the train passengers?"

The driver came over and smiled at her.

"Don't worry, miss. We go back to Lowestoft now, and that's our last trip. Your chap will get a lift like as not. There's been no accident."

Rose nodded her thanks and ran blindly back to Heron's Lodge without really considering what she was going to do next. Bread and milk had been left on the veranda, but when she unlocked the door and went in she hated the emptiness and loneliness. She heard a car coming down the village street and stood stock still wondering if it would stop outside because the driver had given Paul a lift. It did not, but before she could do more she heard a step on the path.

She rushed to the front door to see William.

"Young Paul turned up, Rosie?"

"No, William. No, he wasn't on the bus. What will he do? How will he get home? The trains are all late."

"So we heard from Mrs Buckley who was on the bus. Mary says you're to come back to us and wait. Leave a note for Paul and tell him to come round and pick you up soon as he gets home."

"Oh, William! You're wonderful to me. Fancy you guessing that I would be so worried. Of course I'll come home with you, and we'll leave a note for Paul under the knocker because I must lock up the house again. Are you sure Paul will be all right?"

"Sure, Rosie. He's not a fool and there'll be somebody at the station to give him a lift. Write your note and come along. Has he got a key?"

She nodded and tore a sheet from the pad and wrote,

Bad luck about the late train, Paul. I'm with William and Mary. Please come and fetch me however late you are.

                                                                    Rose.

Back at the cottage, all her fears vanished as Mary fussed over her and gave her a hot drink. They all watched television and it was after ten when the Millers went up to bed.

"Sleep for a while on the sofa," Mary suggested. "Call out if you want anything, but it's a warm night and you can leave the door open and then you'll hear Paul coming."

But she did not hear him and it was after eleven when Paul, out of breath and tired, came hurrying up the path in the moonlight, pushed open the door and saw his sister peacefully sleeping on the Millers' black shiny sofa.

He shook her shoulder none too gently and when she sat up rubbing her eyes and called his name, he said crossly,

"You're a fine sister, I must say. I had to walk from

Blythburgh although I got a lift there in a car. Train was one and a half hours late and how much do you care if I'm starving? And another thing. Why did you leave the door unlocked? It was only by luck that I found your note on the floor in the hall."

"But I'm *sure* I locked the front door and I know that I left the note for you under the knocker. William saw me do it and I thought it would save you unlocking the house. Do you really mean that the door was open?"

"Of course I do. I pushed it while I was fumbling for my key and it opened right away. Buck up and come home, Rose. I've got to have something to eat."

Rose stood up.

"But Paul, don't you see what this means? Somebody else must have been in the house."

4. Harbour Lights

PAUL AND ROSE went to the *Royal Oak* to meet the Halesworth bus the following afternoon. It was full, and the Mortons with a suitcase each and an excited Macbeth on a tartan lead were the last to get off.

"You've made it, then," Paul said rather obviously to David. "Thanks for coming and thanks for telephoning this morning. Sorry about last night but, as I told you, I had to walk most of the way home from the station and Rose was with William and Mary."

"You had me scared," David admitted. "I was glad when you answered the phone this morning. Hello, Rose."

Rose liked David and was glad he was there. She smiled and then turned to the twins.

"Hello, you two. You've brought plenty of luggage. How long are you going to stay?"

Mary turned to her.

"Oh, Rose! It's wonderful to be here and we'll stay as long as you'll have us. David says we've come to help you but we don't know what about yet. He won't tell us . . ."

"Good afternoon, Paul and Rose," said Dickie. "We are in a very polite mood today. That conductor told me just now that courtesy always pays. He was very serious with me and I am now very serious about our manners. We extend to you our salutations, Paul, which is something I read the other day . . . Shall we proceed to your dwelling house with our baggage or shall we go and bathe right away which is what we should like best, if it is all the same to you."

Paul looked astonished and Mary giggled.

"This manners is a new thing with us," she explained. "I don't really think Dickie is very good at it. Do you remember us, Paul?"

"Of course I do, you little idiots. Let's take your luggage home and then we can go on the beach if you like."

David and Dickie were sharing one of the spare rooms at Heron's Lodge and Mary was in with Rose. When the Mortons had unpacked and Macbeth had been given a drink, Rose suggested that if they were going to swim they could take their tea down to the beach. This they did, and an hour later they were lying on their backs with the sun beating down on them.

"We know there's a mystery for us," Mary said suddenly, "David hasn't told us anything really, so you might as well start now. Where's your father, Rose? You haven't said anything about him."

"I know I haven't. He's away, that's why. He'll be back soon, I'm sure. He'll want to see you and before he went he suggested we should ask you, didn't he, Paul?"

"Yes, he did, but the truth is that we don't know where he is," Paul replied. "We may as well tell you everything now, David. Something else happened—or may have happened—last night before I got home."

"I'll tell you," Rose interrupted. "Just listen to me for once instead of to Paul. When I realized that Paul wasn't on the last bus, I went home before I went back to William and Mary's cottage. William had heard about the trains all being late, so I wrote a note to Paul and left it under the knocker of our front door after I'd locked up. Paul says that I only thought I'd locked up, but would I be such a fool as to——"

"O.K., O.K.," Paul interrupted. "They don't know yet what you're making such a fuss about. Just listen. When I got back to Heron's Lodge just about eleven, the front door was unlocked and there *wasn't* a note under the knocker. It was on the floor under the hall table and I was lucky to find it. I thought Rose had gone crackers leaving the door open and I was scared when I realized that the house was empty. Anybody could have walked in."

"So they could! So they could!" Rose shouted triumphantly. "If there is one thing I could swear, twins and

David, it is that I locked that door. I didn't think of it before but of course I can prove it. Ask William Miller! He was there waiting for me, and he saw me lock the door and put the key in the pocket of my jeans. You said anybody could have walked into the house while we were out and I'm sure that my father did. He saw the note, realized the house was empty, unlocked the front door and went in to have a look round and then dropped the note. That's what happened. I'm sure of it. He's got a special reason for wanting to keep all this to himself and we shall know when he's ready to tell us. I'm sure that's the truth."

David and the twins listened to this outburst in silence. It seemed odd that Mr Channing should want to come into his own home without anybody knowing and without even telling his children. Could it possibly be that he had something to hide?

Then Dickie, who never minded speaking out, said, "But why should he, Rose? Of course we don't want you to tell us any private family thing, but you must *know* whether your father came home last night. You were there with Paul later, weren't you? Didn't he leave any clues? Let's go back to your house and look for them."

"And it's no use Paul glaring at my twin like that," Mary added as she got up. "We've come to help you and it seems silly for you and Paul to be squabbling, doesn't it?"

"So it does, Mary," Paul said quietly. "Sorry, Rose. I may as well say straight out that I'm afraid my father is in some sort of trouble, but Rose doesn't think so. We're glad that you three have come, and as Dickie says there ought to be some clues. We slept later this morning because we weren't in bed until about twelve and then there was a bit of tidying up to do, but we didn't see anything suspicious."

"Nothing taken?" David asked. "Rose could be wrong, and it might not have been your father at all. Any food missing?"

"There wasn't really enough to take," Rose laughed. "But it must have been Daddy because he's the only other one to have a key, except Aunt Jane and she's up in Scotland somewhere. You do believe me, don't you, David? Paul asked you to come quickly, specially to help us, but I'm sure that Daddy is just doing something private and that there's not much to worry about."

In spite of her brave words, however, there was a catch in her voice.

"Talk! Talk! Talk!" Dickie said suddenly. "Have you looked in *every* room in the house—every room there is, just to see whether anything has been pinched or whether anybody is still hiding there? Have you?"

Paul looked embarrassed. "I suppose so. No. Not Aunt Jane's room."

"There you are!" Dickie shouted triumphantly. "See what I mean, you Channings? We're on the trail now. And what about your father's room, Rose? Did you look there?"

Rose shook her head. "Daddy doesn't like us going into his bedroom. I didn't look in there, did you, Paul?"

"Come on then," David said. "Let's go and hunt for Dickie's clues. If Rose's friend William saw her lock the front door then it's obvious that someone else with a key must have unlocked it. I believe you, Rose."

So they hurried back to the village as the sun went in and the wind freshened.

Rose raced up the stairs ahead of the others and stopped outside the door of her father's room. None of them laughed or even showed surprise when she lifted her hand and knocked.

They listened in silence but there was no reply and then Paul stepped forward and opened the door.

It was a large room, crammed with big, heavy furniture and looked as if it had been wrecked by a whirlwind. Drawers and wardrobes were open, clothes were all over the place, the bedding was rumpled, although the bed did not look as if it had been slept in.

"I thought so," Rose said quietly. "I told you that Daddy had been back."

Paul turned excitedly to David.

"See what I mean, David? If Father was here last night,

and it looks as if he was, *why did he come in secret and not even leave a message for us?* And what did he want anyway? That's what we've got to find out. Suppose he's going on a journey? What sort of clothes would he need? Why did he have to come back in such a hurry?"

"A journey, Paul? Of course you're right," Rose cried, and ran across the room to a big cupboard and flung back the half-open doors. "Everything here has gone, Paul. All his sailing kit. Oilies and sweaters and sea-boots and everything. He came back for his own kit because he's gone to sea. Has he gone in *Sea Witch*, do you think?"

"Don't you know where your boat is?" David asked.

Paul then explained about their boat, *Sea Witch*.

"You've been in her. She's a seven and a half tonner with an auxiliary engine, but the summer is nearly over and people are already putting their boats up for the winter. Father doesn't keep *Sea Witch* here much and she's at Orford now, down the coast. At least I think she is. He took her down about a fortnight ago, didn't he, Rose?"

"Yes, he did. He asked me if I wanted to go with him but something happened and I didn't. Let's go and ask William whether Daddy mentioned a special sailing trip to him. I'm sure, though, that William doesn't know because he asked me where he was only yesterday, but he *might* have an idea. They've done a lot of sailing together, but I don't think we ought to let William know that Daddy's sailing kit has gone."

"You mean that you don't want people in the village to realize that you don't know where your father is?" David asked.

"It's nobody's business but his," Rose said hotly. "If we ask William not to say anything I'm sure he won't. Come on. Let's go and see him."

On the way to the Millers' cottage, David asked Paul why their boat was kept such a long way off for the winter.

"Better harbour than this. In a big sheltered estuary," Paul explained. "You've never been here in the winter but we have terrible storms. Most of the coast here is being slowly washed away, and when the wind changes to north-west we get real trouble with high tides. There'll be one of the highest tides of the year while you're here—autumn equinox and a full moon. Father likes Orford anyway and often sails there."

William was at home, but although he remembered the Mortons and greeted them with his slow smile, he did not remember Mr Channing saying anything about a special sailing trip. Rose asked him the important question and the others saw that he was suspicious but, when she went on to ask whether he remembered her locking the door of Heron's Lodge last night, he agreed at once that she had done so, and that he had seen her put the note under the knocker.

"But why the fuss?" he asked with a puzzled smile. "No news of Mr Channing, I reckon, after all these questions?"

Before any of them could answer, there was a roar and a spatter of gravel as a green sports car drew up outside.

"It's Mr Wilson again!" Rose called to Mary Miller. "This is a special friend of mine, twins. He's on a London newspaper and he's after a story about some stolen pictures."

"It's James Wilson!" David shouted. "Come on. We know him," and he ran down the path from the cottage door with the twins and Mackie close behind him.

And so it was. Wilson, who was one of the *Clarion's* best reporters, had met the Lone Piners before.*

"Can't escape from you Mortons," he laughed and he shook hands. "Do you mean to tell me that you know my new girl-friend Rose?"

"Yes, of course he does," Rose laughed. "Why have you come back?"

"Wanted to see whether you or Mrs Miller had got any more stories for me about John Jackson. Don't tell me that these twins and David are after J.J. pictures too?"

"We don't know what you are talking about, James," Mary said. "We would like to know but we, too, have a very great mystery to do with, if you know what we mean."

"Just for a moment I'd forgotten that you two talk like

* The Elusive Grasshopper and Lone Pine London.

that. Quite quaint, but I thrive on mysteries. Tell me yours after I've said 'Good afternoon' to Mrs Miller."

Then Paul was introduced, but as soon as Wilson went into the cottage he said, "P'raps somebody will be good enough to tell me something about this smart guy? I don't know what you're talking about, but we don't have to discuss my father with him, surely? You twins had better keep quiet. We don't want our troubles in the newspapers."

The twins looked shocked but, at a warning glance from David, refrained from answering back.

Rose said, "Don't be so foul, Paul. You know they're only trying to help and we're not in real trouble anyway. I'm going to ask Mr Wilson to take us to Orford so that we can find out what's happened to *Sea Witch*."

They all thought that this was a brainwave, and even Paul agreed that it would be better to go and make some inquiries there rather than telephone to the inn at Orford called *Harbour Lights*, where their father sometimes stayed.

When Wilson came back Rose asked him, "If you take that cover thing off the back, could you fit us all in your car and take us to Orford?"

"I suppose I could. I was driving back to London tonight or tomorrow morning because I haven't got much more about J.J. But why Orford? Is this your mystery?"

"Acksherley it is," Mary said. "Please take us, James, and we'll tell you why on the way and you can tell us about this Jackson man you're chasing."

"He's dead, Mary," Wilson laughed. "I'm not chasing him. Let's go for our ride, then. You're all going to be uncomfortable, but we'll try to force you out when we get there. Paul and one of the twins in front with me, and David and Rose in the back with the other terror. Here's Mr and Mrs Miller to see us off."

It was a wonderful ride. The wind tore at their hair and blew back the words when they tried to shout. The sports car roared like a green streak along the straight road crossing the heatherclad common between Walberswick and Blythburgh. Then left, on to the main road, and south through Yoxford and Saxmundham, and then left again towards the coast through Snape and Tunstall and so to Orford with the mighty keep of a Norman castle on a hill and a wonderful church at one end of its broad street.

On the journey, Wilson had little difficulty in persuading Paul to admit that they wanted to know whether Mr Channing had sailed off in *Sea Witch*. He was not told that they believed he had come back to his own house for his sailing kit, but he soon realized that this excitable, highly-strung boy was very anxious about his father. Wilson reasoned that there must be something a little unusual about a man who would go off suddenly, leaving his two children alone even though they had friends staying with them. And it was particularly odd that when he was already chasing up a story about the systematic stealing of John Jackson's pictures in the district where the artist had lived and worked, that he should again meet David Morton and the twins.

Although he had not really got anywhere yet with the J.J. picture business, he still had a hunch that he was on the edge of a story. And there was something out of the ordinary about the Channing family. He had already been captivated by Rose and her loyalty and could understand Paul, but it was not just because he wanted to give all these nice kids a ride that he had brought them to Orford. It was something more. It was that sixth sense that before now had led him to a story. And once again it was to prove right.

He stopped in the central parking place in the broad street and switched off the engine.

"There you are," he smiled. "What next? I don't see a harbour or any sea and I'm thirsty. Where do we go now?"

"You've got to turn round and take the turning to the right," Rose explained. "There isn't actually any sea at Orford, but about a mile down that road there's a harbour with lots of tidal water behind a big shingle bank. You'll see when you get there, but it's a wonderful anchorage in winter for little boats like ours. About half a mile down the road there's an inn called *Harbour Lights*, and we'd like to stop there and ask Bert Hawkins whether he's seen my father. Daddy often stays there."

These directions were simple enough to follow, and a few minutes later they were neatly parked in front of the *Harbour Lights* which was a fair-sized inn with a side entrance to a yard behind the house.

"Bert has four or five bedrooms here and a lounge for residents," Paul explained. "We can all go in although I suppose none of us is allowed in the bar. Will you ask for Mr Channing, please Mr Wilson, if there are other people there? We'll follow you in."

The bar was on the left just inside the front door. It was rather dark, and when they looked in they did not see the stranger sitting in the shadows over by the big fireplace in which a few logs were smouldering.

Wilson walked in, the twins pushed by the others and followed him and suddenly the bar seemed to be full of youngsters who had no right to be there.

Bert Hawkins, a small, sandy man, put down the glass he was polishing and opened his eyes wide with surprise. Before Wilson could say anything, Paul, believing them to be alone with the man they wanted to see, said,

"Hello, Bert. Nice to see you again. We've brought some friends to meet you but we've really come down to see my father. He is staying here, isn't he?"

Hawkins, who was a slow thinker and a slow talker, put down the glass very carefully.

"Now it's a funny thing that you should ask that, Paul. A very funny thing. And how are you, Rose? Good. That's fine. What was I saying? . . . O' course. Your dad? Mr Channing? Now how did you know?"

"Know what, Bert?" Rose said excitedly. "What *do* you mean? *Is* Daddy staying here like he generally does? We want to see him."

"You don't give me a chance to speak, my dear. I was just saying that it's a very peculiar thing that you two should both come in here with your friends asking for your dad."

"*But why, Bert? Why?*"

"Because he ain't here, that's why. He's been in the village but not here. He went out in *Sea Witch* with the tide this afternoon, and I've been wondering whether I done anything to offend him for he's not even looked in to pass the time o' day. And you didn't know where he was? Too bad. Somebody did tell me that this gentleman in the corner went aboard with him . . . Is that so, sir? You know Mr Channing, don't you, sir? He's the father o' these two."

At this the others turned to look at the shadowy figure on the settle by the fire, but almost before Hawkins had finished speaking, the stranger got up hurriedly and went out.

"We've never seen him before, and how do you know that he's been with Daddy?" Rose gasped. "Who is he?"

Before Hawkins could answer, they heard the sound of a car starting up and then coming out of the yard.

"Who is that chap, Bert?" Paul demanded.

"Dunno his name. O.K., though. He came this morning and has paid for all he had and that's all I know."

Wilson ran for the door and out into the street. The others followed, and were just in time to see a big black car disappear towards Orford. Then in the silence, Mary said,

"That man was very, very sinister sitting there in the corner and listening to what we were saying. He had a sort of invisible face, hadn't he? Couldn't see what he was like."

"I could," Wilson said quietly. "I saw him when he hurried out. He reminds me of somebody. No. Maybe he's just somebody fairly well known and I've seen his picture. I think he's been in the news and I must find out who he is. He ran off when he realized that Mr Channing was your father, didn't he, Rose? . . . Very odd . . . I've an idea that he's something to do with pictures and that's very, very interesting. I'll find out. Is your father interested in pictures, Paul?"

Paul shook his head. "Not at all, but let's go down to the harbour now and see whether *Sea Witch* has really sailed, and if she has gone we'd like to know where, wouldn't we?"

5. Bless You, John

On the morning after the events described in the last chapter, the man known as Juan Andrea was once again standing at the open window of his private sitting-room in the *Golden Eagle* hotel in Zutten.

Many local citizens were becoming interested in this over-dressed, smooth-looking man who seemed rather out of place in their busy little town. He never went far and was never away from the hotel for more than an hour or so. But he was well looked after because he paid well. The few questions he asked were in good English, and he expected and got good service. Every day he received several London newspapers, including *The Times*.

It was just after ten o'clock on this particular morning when Andrea saw a small boat coming into the harbour. A smile twitched at the corners of his thin mouth as he read the words *Sea Witch* on her bows. Andrea fetched a pair of binoculars from the mantelpiece and focused them on the man in the boat.

Slowly *Sea Witch* chugged up the harbour and the skipper waved cheerfully to the Harbourmaster who had just come out of his tiny office on the quay to direct him to a suitable berth. The little boat was brought in beautifully and made fast and then the Harbourmaster, in his blue reefer jacket, peaked cap and clogs, went aboard. He was quickly followed by Zutten's Customs Officer dressed rather more officially in a grey-green uniform.

When the three men had gone below, Andrea put down the glasses. He was no longer smiling. This was an anxious moment for he did not like Customs officials, and although he was as sure as he could be that this was the messenger

48

from Donald for whom he was waiting, it was vital, at present, that there should be no obvious connection between the Englishman in *Sea Witch* and himself—particularly if there was to be any trouble between the visitor and the Dutch Customs. He had not liked all that he had read in the British papers recently, although there was also some remarkably good news.

Ah well! He could do nothing now but wait in patience, so he sat down, re-lit his cigar and picked up a copy of *The Times* which was of particular interest to him. He looked first at the column of advertisements in small print headed "Personal" on the back page. The sixth announcement was very short, and read:

Bless you, John. Many happy returns of the 10th.

This was the code message he had been waiting for so impatiently. Today was September 10th and if all went well it was going to be a very important day for him.

Then he picked up another more popular newspaper called *The Clarion* and read, not for the first time, a story headed: THREE J.J. PICTURES STOLEN THIS WEEK.

It was a pity that the British newspapers were making such a fuss about these pictures. Donald was certainly working efficiently and quickly, but perhaps he was too quick? Three J.J.'s already was impressive, but the police of all countries would be on the alert now. How, he wondered, would Donald's messenger, if he could satisfy the Customs, deliver the goods quickly to him? The arrangement was that he should come to the *Golden Eagle* and ask for him in the code arranged. He must be patient, although it might be better to wait downstairs in the lounge rather than up here in his room.

He got up and stubbed out his cigar, surprised to realize that he was feeling nervous. For a moment he delayed looking out of the window, fearing that he might see the Englishman being taken into custody by the police.

He looked out of the window and relaxed.

The Harbourmaster and the Customs Officer were obviously saying a cheerful "Good-bye". Surely he would now come across and make contact and deliver the pictures? Andrea decided to wait for his visitor in the lounge and went downstairs after locking the door of his room behind him.

There were only a few people there and the old waiter in his short white coat approached Andrea as he sat down near the door.

"Good morning. Good day to you, sir. A fine day. May I bring you coffee, sir?"

Andrea nodded. "Upstairs. In my room shortly. Coffee for two. I am waiting for a friend."

Old Jan tried not to show his surprise that this guest should at last have a visitor and hurried into the kitchen to share this remarkable news.

But Andrea's friend did not come, and after a quarter of an hour he got up irritably and went out into the sunshine. He strolled up the quay, well aware that he was looking out of place but determined to discover why Donald's messenger had not kept his appointment. He was not long in doubt, for the skipper of the *Sea Witch* was sleeping peacefully in the sunshine on the deck of his little boat.

Andrea shuddered at the thought that if this man was indeed Donald's messenger, many thousands of pounds' worth of pictures were almost certainly unguarded somewhere aboard. But perhaps the fool had no idea what he was bringing.

He looked at him carefully from the distance of a few yards and was surprised to see that he was rather distinguished looking, and not at all the sort of man whom he thought Donald might have chosen merely to be a carrier and a smuggler of stolen pictures.

Andrea wiped the palms of his hands on a handkerchief of purple silk and walked up and down the quay like a sentry for half an hour until Channing woke, stood up, stretched, glanced at the hotel and then went below.

Andrea was a trifle breathless when old Jan welcomed him again in the lounge.

"My friend comes soon, Jan," he gasped. "Make the

coffee. Bring it up to my room as soon as we have gone up," and he sat down thankfully again near the door.

He was only just in time, for no sooner had Jan shambled off to the kitchen than Channing came in. He had changed his sailing gear and was now wearing a blue shirt and a tweed jacket, but what was much more important to Andrea, he was carrying a black japanned metal case about three feet long and eight inches in diameter. This was, in fact, a case used generally for carrying rolled-up charts.

Andrea got up to greet him and said quietly. "Good morning. Many happy returns of the day."

Channing looked him up and down as if he did not like him very much and then, with rather a sheepish grin, replied, "Bless you, John."

"Upstairs to my room, if you please," Andrea said. "At once, Jan! Bring coffee now."

The waiter plodded up the stairs behind the men and put the tray down on the table. After a curious look at the Englishman he went out and Andrea locked the door behind him.

"Now to business, my friend. I think it wise for us to deal with this matter quickly. How many have you brought? If you want coffee pour it out for yourself."

Channing raised his eyebrows. Who did this chap think he was?

"Come along, my man. Come along. Hand over that case and I will give you a receipt for them."

"Now, listen," Channing said quietly. "I don't know your name and I don't like the way you're speaking to me, but I know you're the chap who wants these charts, and the sooner I get out of here the better I shall like it. I've been paid to bring this to you, neither to ask nor answer any questions, and to get a recipt. I want some sleep so I'm in favour of your suggestion that we waste no time. Where's your receipt?"

"It will be handed over when I am satisfied with what I have received. Pass me that metal case and help yourself to a cigar while I examine the contents."

Channing, after another moment's hesitation, passed over the chart case which was grabbed by Andrea.

"Wait. Wait there, if you please. I will be back," and he went into his bedroom and closed the door.

Channing continued to look very puzzled and unhappy and it was obvious that he had no liking for this errand. He picked up from the coffee tray some of the wrapped cubes of sugar supplied in all Dutch hotels, tossed them in his hand and then unthinkingly slipped them into his pocket. He looked out of the window, fidgeted about and then picked up the copy of the *Clarion* left open on the table by Andrea, and sat down. When he saw the reproduction of Jackson's "Red Mill" and read James Wilson's story under the staring banner head-line, he sat back as if stunned. Then he crumpled up the newspaper, strode across the room and flung back the bedroom door.

Andrea was standing by the window with the canvas of the "Red Mill" between his hands. On the bed was the metal chart case, several genuine Admiralty charts and another J.J. picture.

The two men stared at each other in malevolent silence.

"I told you to keep out, didn't I? Keep away. Can't you understand me?"

"I'm understanding a lot—for the first time. Seems as if I've been a fool. I didn't know I was being paid to work for what looks like a picture racket. Donald has made a fool of me. I knew he had some odd tricks up his sleeve but I didn't think he was a criminal. Now I'm sure he is and I'm going to do something about it . . ."

Andrea paled.

"Don't be a fool, man! Don't be a fool. Donald trusts you —he told me so himself. You're in this as much as we are so just try to be sensible and listen to me."

"I don't want to listen to you. I don't know your name but I don't like you. You wouldn't understand, but I knew that crazy chap Jackson who painted those pictures. He was a great man and that mill is near my home. I've a good mind to knock you down but maybe it's not quite the time. I've got to think what's the best thing to do."

Andrea pulled a thick leather wallet from his pocket.

"Now listen. Just be sensible. Maybe Donald didn't pay you enough? Let us do a leetle deal together. I'm going to ask you to accept a leetle present and then you will forget that you ever saw inside this metal case with the—what do you call them? The maps. Of course . . . You can go back to England, give Mr Donald the receipt that I have here for you and forget the pictures. Here! To please me you will accept this leetle present."

And to Channing's astonishment he threw on to the bed a bundle of £10 notes.

There was a long pause. Then, "You can keep your money," Channing said quietly. "To offer me that was one of your bigger mistakes. I'm going to have plenty of time and opportunity to think what I am going to do," and he picked up the receipt and the charts, put the latter in the metal case, walked with it through the sitting-room, unlocked the door and slammed it behind him.

Andrea thrust the two precious canvasses under some silk shirts at the bottom of a drawer and ran to the window. What was this man going to do now? It was clear that he had had no knowledge of what he was smuggling into Holland and was shocked by the discovery. Worse, he was almost certainly the only man to know of the association between Donald and himself and was therefore doubly dangerous. What would he do? Go to the Customs? Go to the Dutch police? Sail back to England and give them away? He seemed to be the sort of fool who would confess what he himself had done just for the principle of exposing the plot. *What would he do?*

There he was now. Striding down the quay with the chart case under his arm and not even looking where he was going. Was he going aboard *Sea Witch* or going to the Harbourmaster's office?

Andrea sighed with relief when Channing jumped aboard the little boat and went below. But his relief was short-lived for there was no doubt that both he and Donald were in this man's power.

In sudden panic Andrea reached for the telephone and impatiently jiggled the receiver rest to call the hotel's switchboard.

"Quickly!" he shouted. "Urgent! I want London. Give me London."

6. The Chestnuts

WHERE THE NORTHERN suburbs of London sprawl out between the hills of Highgate and Barnet is the area known as Finchley. And the most respectable of all Finchley's avenues is probably that called Hastings Avenue. The fourth house on the right hand side coming from the main road is *The Chestnuts*. There is nothing remarkable about its appearance but its owner could probably buy up every other house in the Avenue. His name is Simon Donald, and he lives here alone with an elderly housekeeper named Mrs Brian and is something of a mystery to his neighbours.

Although Donald has an office and a picture gallery in the West End of London, he often works in his study at *The Chestnuts* when he does not wish to be disturbed. The Mr Donald of Finchley is somehow not quite the same man as the picture dealer of Bond Street. Those who know his reputation as an art expert would be amazed if they could see *The Chestnuts*—an ordinary, detached villa in an unexciting suburb. But perhaps that is why Mr Donald lives there?

At the same time that Juan Andrea was grabbing the telephone in his hotel at Zutten, Mr Simon Donald was sitting at his desk in his study. The desk had nothing on it but a pad of pink blotting-paper and the telephone, and the most unusual thing in the room besides a framed landscape on the wall was a big green safe.

Mr Donald looked just as ordinary as when we first met him in Holland and was glancing at his wrist-watch when the telephone rang. Donald rarely raised his voice, and when the operator had confirmed his number and said, "Hold on, please. Holland wants you," all he said was, "Thank you. Put them through, if you please."

Then, "This is Simon Donald. Who wants him?"

Such a torrent of sound followed that Donald held the instrument distastefully a few inches from his ear.

"Listen, Donald. This is 'Bless you, John' speaking. Can you hear me? This is what you call urgent and private. Are you there?"

"I am here. Calm yourself. I told you not to telephone unless there was an emergency . . . What has happened, and be guarded in what you say. Has my messenger arrived?"

"Yes, yes. He has come. That is the trouble."

"Well, tell me. Have you got what he brought?"

"Yes. Yes. I have them. That is well enough, but the man is what you call crazy. He threatens us. He did not know what he was doing but now he find out."

Donald frowned. There was no doubt that Andrea was excited because he was losing his command of English. It was going to be difficult to keep him to the point, and what was this nonsense about Channing?

"Tell me quickly what you mean, Andrea. Where is my messenger now?"

"On his boat. It is called *Sea Witch* and I can see it from my window here. Listen. Now that he knows what he was carrying he is very angry. He threatens you and me too. All I know is that he has not yet gone to the police but he may do so. You will be wise to be the first to meet your messenger on his return to England. It will be important for him to speak to nobody but you. *Nobody at all.* He might go to the police in your country. You will know best what to do because he is your man and not mine. *But do not let him go to the police* and do not send anything more for me until I say. I will write to tell you where you will find me if I stay no longer here. You will not forget. Now I go."

There was a click and Donald found himself for once without words to reply even if it had been possible to do so.

Was it likely that he had really misjudged Channing? He knew him as a happy-go-lucky, lazy man whom he had once got out of some trivial trouble and who, since then, had always been ready to help him for payment.

Donald had people working for him in all parts of Britain

and in many European countries too. Not one living person besides Donald knew what was in the big safe in this room. Pictures were not his only business, and Channing had previously been useful to him in getting introductions to important people in East Anglia and occasionally by acting as an unsuspecting carrier of stolen goods.

In this matter of the J.J. pictures Donald had offered him a big fee for delivering a case of charts to Zutten, knowing that Channing would almost certainly rise to the bait of an exciting, one-man trip across the North Sea. This was a risk he had been prepared to take. Channing, with his free and easy manner, could get away with anything if he did not know the truth.

But now he had found out, and Donald saw at once that Andrea was right in suggesting how dangerous Channing could be. And what was it he had said? *"You will know best what to do because he is your man and not mine."*

Donald pressed a bell-push in the wall. An elderly woman came quietly into the room and stood just inside the door. She looked like a prosperous country woman with rosy cheeks and smoothly parted white hair.

"Ah! Mrs Brian! Thank you. I will have my lunch here, on a tray, if you please. Then for at least two hours I shall be busy on the telephone and am not to be disturbed. Later this evening I shall be travelling to Suffolk by car, and shall be glad if you will pack suitable clothes for a visit to the country."

"Certainly, Mr Donald. Can you suggest how long your stay will be."

He looked up at her without speaking. What an excellent woman she was. Never, since she had come to *The Chestnuts* six years ago, had she given him or anybody else the slightest hint that he was anything more than a respected picture dealer with a West End gallery. She was, indeed, the perfect housekeeper, but she was paid just four times as much as an ordinary housekeeper!

"Pack for a fortnight's stay, please, Mrs Brian," Donald replied.

When he had finished his meal and Mrs Brian had left

him with his coffee, he took from the shelves a big atlas and
opened it at the page showing France with the Low
Countries and the southern and eastern coasts of Britain.

Zutten was opposite Felixstowe. He then turned to a
bigger map of the East Coast and tried to put himself in
the place of Channing who might, even now, be on his way
back to England. It seemed likely that he would return to
Orford, for he could not have had much sleep in the last
twenty-four hours and so would choose the shortest route.
All depended on the wind and tide, of course, but he could
soon get news of those.

Donald looked carefully at the map, and with a pencil
wrote down a list of those places where Channing might
land. Great Yarmouth seemed too far north but Lowestoft
was possible. Southwold and Walberswick sharing the same
little harbour up the river Blyth were probable. Then
Aldeburgh to the north of Orford might have attractions,
but if he sailed farther south to Bardsey or Felixstowe or
Harwich or even Brightlingsea or Burnham he would be
difficult to welcome. This was going to be a more exacting
task than he had first thought. And time was short.

He put away the atlas, unlocked the big safe and brought
from it a thin, leather-bound address book. With this before
him he sat at his desk and began to use the telephone. He
was still using it one and a half hours later—quietly and
decisively giving his orders to a number of men and women
in his pay. It was not possible, at such short notice, to
cover every port on the East Coast, but before he had
finished, members of his organization were already con-
verging on those places most likely to be used by Channing.

Donald's orders were clear. Channing's appearance was
carefully described and so was *Sea Witch*. His house in
Walberswick was to be watched and *under no circumstances*
was he to be allowed to go home, to telephone or contact the
police. *He must be picked up within the next twenty-four hours* and
reports were to be made to Donald in the furnished house
he had taken between Southwold and Walberswick a few
weeks ago.

Each of the telephone conversations had finished like this, "This man is a danger to us all—make no mistake about that. I must see him before he gets to his home, to a hotel or even to a telephone. I shall be personally in charge in Southwold before midnight. Report back, remembering that watch must be kept on all the ports through the night. Repeat my Southwold telephone number, please."

When the last message had been sent and the last pencil note made on his list, he folded the latter into his address book and put it in his pocket. Then he sent for some tea and while he was enjoying it the telephone rang. When, without thinking or waiting for Mrs Brian to answer it on the instrument in the hall, he lifted the receiver, he made his second big mistake in the affair of the J.J. pictures.

As soon as he had announced his number, a man's pleasant voice said, "Good afternoon, Mr Donald. This is the *Clarion* speaking and we hope you will favour us with an exclusive interview for tomorrow's paper. What, in your opinion, is the reason for this sudden craze for the pictures of John Jackson? Why should they so have increased in value during the last year or two?"

For a fraction of a second Donald wondered whether to replace the receiver and cut short the conversation but just in time he realized that this might be considered a suspicious action. The people who work on newspapers are clever.

He replied, "I'm sorry, young man, but I do not give interviews and you would be wasting your time if you came out here to see me. I am just leaving for a holiday."

"But perhaps now, sir, you could give me your personal opinion on the Jackson pictures? You will realize that we must give our readers the opinions of experts. These thefts in different parts of the country of J.J. landscapes are creating a great deal of interest. Will their value rise, do you think? Is the work of this little-known and until now unappreciated artist becoming popular in America and in European countries? Jackson's work is typically British, is it not?"

Donald replied coolly and politely, giving some general views on the importance of the artist's work.

"Thank you, Mr Donald. I should have liked to have talked to you personally but am grateful for what you've said. Are you going abroad? We might want to speak to you again . . . I see. Touring. That does make it difficult . . . Should you wish to express any more views, perhaps you'd telephone me at the *Clarion* . . . My name is Wilson."

Twenty minutes later, Donald was driving into Hastings Avenue. Mrs Brian stood in the porch watching him. She was not likely to forget his last words to her.

"You are now entirely responsible for what happens here, Mrs Brian. Take a careful note of all telephone calls, but nobody is to be given my Southwold number unless the caller is one of us and known to us both. You will please open the post daily and report to me every four hours during each day that I am away. If there is no reply from Southwold, you must continue to ring at say half-hourly intervals until I answer. My Suffolk address is not to be disclosed to anyone unless you ask me first. You know Channing because he has been here several times, but he is the man I want. Should he ring here, *find out where he is* and say that you can find me and will ask me to meet him as soon as possible. Use your wits, Mrs Brian. He must be kept quiet and unsuspicious until we can get to him . . . And if a glib young man from the *Clarion*—or anyone from any other newspaper —rings up or calls, keep them sweet, but say I am touring and cannot be reached. *But I shall want to know which newspapers are asking for me* . . . Thank you, Mrs Brian. That is all."

It was not until he was through Colchester that he remembered something very important.

Those children! A pack of children coming into the *Harbour Lights* with a strange man. And two of them were Channing's children, and the innkeeper had told them that their father had sailed off in *Sea Witch*. Suddenly it was obvious that Channing was keeping his own secrets from his own children and that they were now searching for him. Now, not only must he prevent Channing from communicating with anybody, but he must make sure that his children and their friends did not trace him either.

7. *Sea Witch Comes Home*

DURING THE DAY that Andrea telephoned to London and Simon Donald drove through the evening to Southwold, the children at Heron's Lodge did little more than argue and irritate each other. By the time it was dark the weather had changed and the wind howled round the old house. Eventually the twins went off to bed followed by Rose.

When David and Paul were alone, the former went over to the window and drew back the curtains. With his back to Paul he said, "This hasn't been much of a day, has it? We're not helping you, Paul, and I think we'd better go back to London tomorrow unless we can get this sorted out quickly. You're just waiting for something to turn up. You're scared for your father and you won't even tell me all that you're afraid of, will you?"

Paul shook his head.

"No, I won't. I'm not sure what I'm scared of, but I'm sorry we've made a mess of today. I don't want you to go home and neither will Rose. Let's wait until the morning and see whether there's anything in the post from my father. We might get a message. Sometimes I wonder whether Rose is right and that we've got nothing to fear."

*   *   *

There was nothing of any importance in the post next morning, and although the sun was not shining and the wind was blowing hard, they were all more cheerful at breakfast. When Paul had glanced at the three envelopes and put them with the other letters waiting for Mr Chaning, David looked up. "If you got a message from your father, Paul, you promised that we'd do something today.

61

We can't sit about doing nothing. Let's make a plan. You do see don't you, Rose, that we can't wait any longer?"

She stared out of the window. "Yes. I'm frightened now because he hasn't written or telephoned . . ."

Dickie interrupted.

"I know what to do. We've done it before. Let's go back to the day before yesterday and remember everything that happened when James Wilson took us in that super car to Orford and we saw the man in the black car. I wish we'd seen the number of that one."

So as they cleared up their breakfast they tried to recall everything that had happened after the car had driven off as soon as its unknown occupant realized that Paul and Rose were asking for their father. The innkeeper, Hawkins, had not been able to tell them any more, but Wilson had driven them down to the quay where they had questioned an old fisherman. He had not been the brightest of old men but he knew Mr Channing and *Sea Witch*, and had seen a stranger in a big, black car drive up and go aboard with him for about ten minutes. He had been carrying a metal chart case.

Rose remembered well that she had asked the old man whether her father had looked well and happy.

"And he said that yes, he did. Don't you remember? If he was well and happy then I don't suppose we have to worry much, do you? P'raps I'm silly now but if I am it's because you're all so gloomy. P'raps I'm not frightened any more."

"I expect you're right, Rose," Mary said loyally. "All the same it would be wonderful for us all if we knew where your father had gone, wouldn't it? Can anybody remember what James said after we'd found out about *Sea Witch* going off?"

"Yes, I remember," David said. "He asked the old boy whether Mr Channing had said how long he would be at sea and where he was going."

"True enough," Paul put in. "And he said Father hadn't told him anything and I'm not surprised at that."

They remembered then that Wilson had not said much else to them before going back to London, beyond a suspicion that the stranger they had seen in the bar of the *Harbour Lights* had reminded him of somebody in the news—somebody connected with pictures.

"He should have telephoned us yesterday," Paul said. "He promised to ring if he found out anything."

"Never mind that now," David replied. "We can ring him presently. I was thinking this over last night when the wind kept me awake and I want to say this. We know now that Mr Channing is by himself, but he can't have gone very far single-handed, can he? He's got to eat and sleep."

"Of course he has," Rose cried. "But he's so good on *Sea Witch*, David."

"Maybe," David agreed. "But you're both worried and it's no use pretending you're not. He might have had an accident, and don't you think you ought to tell the police—or your Aunt Jane?"

A long silence followed this outrageous suggestion.

Then, "Aunt Jane?" Rose protested. "You met her once, didn't you? If you'll think you'll realize how silly you are. Anyway, we can't find her now, and if we told George, our local policeman, Daddy would never, never forgive us . . . If that's the only thing you can suggest, David, then I think you're—you're absolutely hopeless . . . Anyone might think my father is dead or something," and with a strangled sob she ran out of the room followed by the twins and Macbeth.

"Now see what you've done," Paul said gloomily. "Let her go. Let them all go. If you're going to telephone Wilson in London, why don't you do it now? What really worries me, David, is the chap who went off in that car as soon as he heard that we were asking for Father. He was the man who saw him on *Sea Witch* before coming back to *Harbour Lights*. And he's the chap who reminds Wilson of somebody he knows. Now that the others are out of the way, can't you see that's what scares me in this business? Is he the man Father goes off to see in London? Why should he go aboard with him with a chart case? Father's been away nearly a week now, David, but of course we can't go to the police."

David shrugged his shoulders and went to the door.

"O.K., Paul. I only hope you won't have to tell them later. I'll ring up *The Clarion* now."

The telephone was in the sitting-room, and as Paul followed him down the hall neither of the boys realized that the house was quiet and that there was no sign of Rose or the twins. They closed the door behind them, and while David got through to London, Paul stood close to him so that he could overhear the conversation.

Wilson was in *The Clarion* office.

"Mr James Wilson?" David asked. "Hello, James! This is David Morton from Walberswick."

"Yes, David. Any news? Has Mr Channing turned up?"

"No. We're all very worried. Why didn't you telephone us yesterday? We waited in all day."

"Sorry, David. I was busy. Why are you telephoning now? Are you sure that *Sea Witch* hasn't come back?"

"Not as far as we know. Did you find out about that man who was in the pub at Orford and who drove off in a hurry? You said he reminded you of somebody in the news."

"Yes. I found him. His name is Simon Donald and he's a well-known picture dealer with galleries in the West End of London and a house in Finchley. I telephoned him yesterday for a story about the J.J. pictures but didn't get much out of him. He was just off for a touring holiday."

"Oh, was he, James? Didn't you ask him what he was doing at Orford day before yesterday? We know now that he must be something to do with Mr Channing."

Here there was a considerable pause and when Wilson answered his cheerful voice held a note of respect.

"That's quite an idea, David, but it did occur to me too. Actually I went up to Finchley last night but there was only a respectable housekeeper there. Anyway Mr Donald's car was not in his garage, because he'd left the doors open . . . Thank you for ringing, David, and I may be up again soon. If Mr Channing turns up, telephone here or at the flat, at once, please. Same if you see Donald, although I can't see why he should want to come your way again. If I'm not here, leave a message for me to ring you. I'm just off on another story but I'll try and get over to Finchley soon and have a look round."

David frowned as he put down the receiver.

"You heard all that, Paul! I don't like it. There's some connection between this man Donald and your father, and perhaps if we could find the first we'll find the second too . . . I still think that we should tell the police."

"That's ridiculous. We know he sailed in *Sea Witch* day before yesterday. He hasn't been away any time."

"Perhaps not, but he didn't tell you when or where he was going and that's what is worrying me now as much as you. Let's see what those kids are doing."

But a scribbled note on the hall table told them that Rose and the twins had gone.

Don't worry about us. We are fed up with you not doing anything and have gone to Orford. Rose is very unhappy and we are helping her. You two don't do anything but talk.

"Let them go," Paul said. "They won't find out anything there."

But he was wrong.

* * *

Rose, Dickie and Mary, with Macbeth racing excitedly beside them, ran for the bus as soon as David began to use the telephone. They did not notice a young, red-headed woman in a belted raincoat watching them from the other side of the road. Why should they? She looked just like any other holiday-maker on this cool and stormy morning.

They only just caught the bus and it was several minutes before they recovered enough breath to speak to each other.

"This bus only takes us to Blythburgh," said Rose, "But we'll get lifts and get to Orford somehow. Tide's just about full now and I bet Daddy has come in with it. He'll be thrilled to see us . . . Yes, he will, twins."

At last, after two buses and a lift in a baker's van, they reached Orford. The van swept past the *Harbour Lights* before they could even see whether any cars were in the yard, and then a few minutes later drew up at the cottages just by the water. Almost before the driver had stopped, Rose jumped out and as the others followed, after shouting their thanks, she stopped and pointed to a boat moored to the quay.

"He's home!" she whispered. "He's come home! That's *Sea Witch*. Now everything will be all right."

But there was nobody aboard and it did not take long to be sure of that! But in the tiny cabin there was a smell of pipe tobacco, a muddle of dirty dishes and every sign that Channing—or some other man—had been there not long ago.

"But where has he gone?" Rose cried. "Someone must have seen him. Let's find Adam."

As they jumped ashore the old fisherman came out of his cottage and waved to them.

"*Please*, Adam. Please have you seen my father?" Rose begged. "When did *Sea Witch* come in?"

"Not more'n hour ago, miss. I seen your Dad. He was a-yawnin' his head off. Reckon he's gone up to *Harbour Lights* for a snooze. I can't hear as well as some, and folk talk softer these days but he ask me to keep an eye on her."

"Thank you, Adam. We'll go and find Daddy now."

Rose ran so fast back to the inn that the twins had difficulty in keeping up with her, and they hardly had enough breath left to speak when they arrived. Bert Hawkins came out of the bar when he heard them.

"Steady, Rose. Steady, girl," he said when she clung to his hand. "What's fussing you now? How did you get here?"

"In a baker's van," Mary said. "*Sea Witch* has come home, and we want to know if Mr Channing is here."

"Sure he is. Upstairs in Number Three and fast asleep by now. 'Not to be disturbed', he said, and you'd best let him have his sleep out, Rose. He was whacked and you must give him an hour or two."

"But is he all right? Did he say where he'd been? Did he telephone us at home? Did he ask for us?"

"No, Rosie. No, he didn't. Just said he wanted a room and a bed and wasn't to be disturbed. Shall I give him a message from you when he comes down?"

"Of course not, Bert. We'll soon be back so that we're here when he wakes up. We'll go back now and tidy up *Sea Witch* so that he doesn't have to do any more than collect his gear when he's ready to go. If he does come down before we're back of course you can tell him where we are . . . 'Bye, Bert, and thank you."

They walked back slowly to the quay feeling very much more cheerful. Mary let Macbeth off his lead, and the little dog frisked along happily sniffing the wind which was blowing strongly from the sea.

It was Mary who made the important discovery five minutes later when helping Rose to clear up the muddle on the folding table in *Sea Witch*'s cabin. Beside a thick, white china mug containing the dregs of cold coffee were some little packets of cube sugar enclosed in printed paper wrappings. Near by were two other rumpled papers from which the sugar had been taken.

Mary picked them up curiously. There were words in a strange language and a drawing of what looked like a bird's head on each paper.

"Look, Rose! Come down here, Dickie, and see the clue I've found. It's a real clue, and if you know the language of these words you'll know where your father has been, Rose. What does it mean?"

Dickie jumped down from the deck where he had been teasing Macbeth while Rose picked up one of the papers.

"It's German, Mary. Or could be Flemish or Dutch. I think it means 'Golden Eagle Hotel' at a place called Zutten. I s'pose Daddy could have sailed to Belgium or Holland and back in the time? Germany is too far for him to sail by himself. He loves a lot of sugar in his coffee, but it doesn't really matter, does it, because we shall see him soon and he'll tell us everything."

The twins looked at her in surprise, and the silence that followed was broken by the sound of heavy footsteps on the quay and then Macbeth's frenzied barking as a man jumped down on to the deck.

Mary was the first up from the cabin as the stranger shouted at the dog, "Shut up, you!" She disliked anybody who shouted at or tried to bully Macbeth. So did Dickie, but the three children would have hated this man on sight even if he had made a fuss of the dog.

He was short and thickset and wearing a double-breasted blue suit. In one hand he carried a cap with a shiny peak and Mary guessed that he was a chauffeur. His hair was straw-coloured and close-cropped, and his grey eyes hard and cruel.

"Who are you?" Rose demanded. "How dare you bully our dog. This isn't your boat. Please go away."

The man's cold eyes regarded them unsmilingly.

"Keep that dog out of the way else I'll throw him in the water," he said. "I'm looking for Mr Channing. I want him urgent. This boat is his."

"Why do you want him? Tell us who you are and what you want to say to him? I'll give him a message."

Mary glanced quickly at her twin who was trying to hold the struggling Macbeth in his arms. She was suddenly uneasy, with the feeling that they were in great danger. She looked ashore but nobody was in sight and if this man was a chauffeur, where was his car? From where had he so suddenly appeared? How could she make Dickie understand that they would be safer off *Sea Witch*? Perhaps they could run for it, although Rose, flushed with indignation, was still standing up to the bully who was now glaring at them with one hand clenched in the pocket of his jacket.

Dickie returned her glance, looking slightly puzzled, but before he could speak the man said, "How can you give him a message? Who are you?"

"I'm his daughter," Rose flared. "You've no right on *Sea Witch*. Get off. I'm in charge here."

The man's expression changed and Mary was sure that Rose had made a mistake by saying who she was. "Where's your father, kids? Where is he? Tell me quickly because

I've got an urgent message for him. Where's Channing?"

Then Dickie made a mistake, too.

"You go and boil your head somewhere else!" he shouted as he put Mackie down on the deck. "We're not afraid of you. Anyway you can't see Mr Channing. He won't want to see you. He's tired and he's not to be disturbed."

There was a long silence, broken first by Mackie who crouched with his head on his forepaws and growled menacingly. Mary bent down and grabbed him by the collar. Then she dragged him backwards so that she was between the man and the quay which was now about two feet above her because the tide was ebbing fast.

The others sensed what Mary was trying to do as the man stepped forward and shouted, "So he's not to be disturbed, eh? So you know where he is . . . ? Come here, you cheeky little devil," and he grabbed at Dickie and caught him a glancing blow on the head. The boy put a hand to his face and dodged to his sister's side as she released Macbeth.

"At him, boy," she whispered. "See him off," and then to Rose, "We've got to run, Rose. Get ashore and help us up."

Macbeth, a snarling, bristling little black fury, went into battle. Their enemy backed and lashed out again at the dog with his foot. Then he brought something that gleamed in his clenched hand out of his jacket pocket, but before he could strike, Mackie bit him on the ankle. With a curse the man backed into the gunwales, stumbled, waved his arms wildly and then disappeared over the side of *Sea Witch* with a resounding splosh.

Macbeth, with triumphantly waving tail and a bark of victory, tried to follow him but Mary grabbed him back. Over her shoulder she saw that Rose was now on the quay helping Dickie up beside her.

Then she looked down and saw below her the pink-faced bully floundering and swearing in two feet of water and black, slimy mud.

"Quick, Mary. Quickly! Hand up Mackie."

Two minutes later the three of them, with Macbeth gambolling at their heels, were racing up the road towards the inn. Twice they looked back over their shoulders but there was no sign of the chauffeur. No pursuit.

They trotted on together and three minutes later, when they turned the corner, they were in time to see a big black car turn out of the yard of the *Harbour Lights*, accelerate quickly and disappear round the corner.

"Wonder who that is?" Dickie puffed. "I bet our chauffeur wishes he was in that. Bet he wishes he wasn't drowned!"

But Rose was not listening. She had raced ahead, and when the twins reached the inn she was already talking excitedly to Bert Hawkins in the doorway.

"But, Bert, you *must* believe me. He had a chauffeur's cap in his hand and came aboard *Sea Witch* and began to bully us and ask for Daddy. He fell over the side when Mackie bit him and he might be drowned. P'raps he belonged to the big black car that's just driven off? Who was in that? And is Daddy awake yet? I must go and tell him what has happened."

Bert Hawkins was not a man who liked trouble or argument, and he now sensed that he was getting mixed up in something not quite straightforward. He liked Mr Channing and the children but all this talk of chauffeurs falling off boats was too much.

"Now you just stop fussing, my dear, and pipe down. There's been no chauffeur round here so far as I know and anyway your chap won't drown in a foot of water. There's only one asked for your dad and he's up with him now."

"Who's up with him?" Rose cried. "He said he wasn't to be disturbed. Who was in the car that drove off just now . . . *Bert! Please listen and answer me!*" and she clutched his arm and looked up at him with tears in her eyes.

He told them then. Soon after they had gone, the man who had been in the bar the day on which *Sea Witch* sailed came into the inn. Bert did not actually see the car or a chauffeur, but the man was pleasant enough and asked casually for Channing.

"I told him what I told you, Rose. Said your dad had come in early and was sleeping upstairs and wasn't to be disturbed, but he said he must see him right away and I wasn't to worry and he'd make it O.K. with him. So what was I to do? I was in the kitchen so I didn't hear the car go just now, and for all I know your dad is still up there . . . What's wrong, Rose?"

"I wish I knew!" she sobbed. "I'm going up to find my father. What room did you say he was in? Come with me, twins—Mackie too."

Bert shrugged his shoulders in despair.

"First on the right on the first landing. Number Three—and don't blame me if he's mad with you."

Dickie looked back at him from half-way up the stairs.

"If that drowned chauffeur comes here asking for us, you must jolly well swear that you've never seen us until we've told Mr Channing all about it."

By now Rose was knocking at the door of Number Three. There was no reply and no sound from within the room. She opened the door, remembering as she did so how only two days ago she had knocked on the door of her father's bedroom, at home in Heron's Lodge.

This room was empty too, although the bed-clothes were tumbled. Rose wheeled on the others standing in the doorway and they saw the tears on her face.

"He's gone again, twins. I can never find him. Why doesn't he tell us where he is?"

Then she saw the landlord standing behind the twins.

"Tell me the truth, Bert! Did he ask for me? Did you tell him we'd been here and were coming back for him because we didn't want to disturb him? *Did you tell him?*"

"No, my dear. I didn't see him go, so I couldn't tell him."

"And what about the man who came to see him? Did you tell him we'd been here?"

Bert shook his head and then, before he could answer, they all heard an angry voice shouting from downstairs.

"Isn't there anybody to give service in this place? I want a hot bath in a hurry. And where's the car I brought here? And has anybody here seen three saucy kids with a dog?"

"Coming, sir!" Bert called, and then in a whisper to the

children, "Quietly down this passage. Through the closed door at the end you'll find stairs leading down to the kitchen. Tell the missus what I said and that I'm looking after that chap. Don't worry, Rosie. I'll see you through this. Come back later if I can help. Or ring up. There's a bus in ten minutes."

Macbeth growled softly and Mary begged him to keep quiet as she picked him up. Then together they left the empty room and tip-toed down the passage and opened the door leading to the kitchen stairs.

"Pity!" Dickie whispered hoarsely as he closed it gently behind him. "Pity, he didn't drown."

8. The Girl with Red Hair

DAVID LAUGHED as he put down the note scribbled by Rose before she had gone off to Orford with the twins.

"I don't really blame them, Paul. Anyway, we can't do much about it. I suppose a bus has just gone and Rose knew we couldn't catch them . . . Why don't we go to Southwold? If we stay here we shall only get on each other's nerves. Haven't you got a dinghy down at the harbour? We needn't be away for long, and you can always ring up here from Southwold to see if any of them have come back."

Paul nodded. "Good idea. If Father is coming home today, like as not he'll be in on this tide. Let's go down to the harbour now."

They were half-way to the front gate when they heard the telephone ringing. Paul ran back, unlocked the front door and went into the sitting-room while David waited in the road. He returned looking worried.

"Your friend James Wilson again. He was in a hurry and asked me to tell you that he's coming back here to Walberswick tonight. Says he's telephoned that chap Donald's house at Finchley again."

"Was Donald there? Why didn't you call me, Paul?"

"I've told you. He was in a hurry. Donald's housekeeper said that he was away, that she didn't know where he was or when he would be back. Wilson says he's now sure that Donald is the man we saw at the pub in Orford."

"But why should a picture dealer know your father, Paul? And why is James coming back here in such a hurry?"

"He didn't say. Come on, let's go."

They continued along the road, but on their way to the river were stopped by Mrs Miller at her cottage gate.

"Good morning to you both. I was thinking of coming along to Heron's Lodge to see if any of you were about. Have you any news of your father, Paul?"

"Not a word, Mary. Has *Sea Witch* come in on the tide?" Mrs Miller buttoned up her cardigan against the wind.

"No, Paul," she said quietly. "*Sea Witch* hasn't come in with the tide. I'd like you two boys to come inside for a minute for I've something to tell you. Have you spoken to any strangers since you've been out this morning?"

They both shook their heads and then looked at each other wonderingly as they followed her indoors. She closed the door and then looked out of the window towards the river before she spoke.

"Maybe I'm wrong to be as worried about your father as you are, Paul. Tell me straight, now. Do you know when he's coming back or where he is?"

"No, I do not. You know I don't, and I'm sick and tired of this mystery. Why are you worried, Mary? What's happened now? What do you want to tell us?"

"There's too many strangers round here interested in Mr Channing," Mrs Miller said soberly. "There was that newspaper rascal, and this morning—not more'n an hour since —there's this red-headed girl."

"Girl? What girl?" Paul asked.

"Give me a chance and I'll tell you, Paul. She's pretty in a bold sort o' way. About twenty maybe, but it is difficult to tell these days. I reckoned at first she was a holiday visitor from Southwold, but she came over alone in the ferry and visitors aren't often alone. I watched her come up the path from the river, and as this is the first house in Walberswick she walks up and knocks on the door."

She paused for breath and David asked,

"Sure you've never seen her before?"

"No. I'm sure of that. Pretty she was and wishes me time of day civil enough, and then asks straight out whether I've seen a little boat called *Sea Witch* come into harbour last two days! You can guess I was surprised at this and you'd be right . . . No, I said. *Sea Witch* hadn't been in and why did she want to know? Then she said that she had an urgent message for Mr Channing and did I know when he'd be back. O' course I didn't, and having got my wits again I asked why she thought I should know. At that she gave me rather a saucy smile and said she'd go on up to Heron's Lodge to see if anyone there knew anything about him. That's why I asked whether you'd seen any strangers this morning. Has she been to Heron's Lodge? It's more'n an hour ago since she was here and she went up to the village and came back about ten minutes before you. She's either gone on the ferry or is down by the river. Have you seen her, Paul?"

He shook his head.

"Don't think so. There are visitors about, of course. We didn't see anybody special at home. I don't know anybody like this girl. How does she know about Father?"

"I don't know, Paul. I don't know. Why should a girl like that be wanting to give him an urgent message? How did she know the name of your house?"

"Somebody Father knows round here may have sent her with a message," Paul suggested. "Don't worry, though. If she comes back, say we'll be home about tea-time. We're going to Southwold and will look out for her."

"No, don't tell her when we'll be back," David said quickly. "I'm sure we shouldn't let anybody know that the house is empty. Just say you don't know anything, Mrs Miller, but try to find out all you can about her."

So they said "Good-bye" and went down to the river.

Below them, three dinghies were moored to the narrow, ramshackle landing stage used by the ferry, but the actual ferry boat was on the other side of the river. And sitting on the shore end of the little stage was a red-headed girl.

"There you are, Paul," David said quietly. "She's waiting for you. Must be you she wants. Shall I go?"

"Don't be a fool! I'm sure I've never seen her before, but as we're going over in our dinghy which is moored almost under her feet, let's see what she has to say for herself."

"If you want the ferry I'm afraid nothing is happening,"

the girl smiled at Paul. "Nobody takes any notice of my signals of distress. Are you going across to Southwold? I suppose we couldn't borrow one of these little boats? Do you live here? Isn't it a horrid morning?"

David was at once suspicious and thought her much too bright and chatty.

"I'm just a summer visitor," he said brightly. "You on holiday too? I haven't seen you about on the beach. It's funny how you get to know people when you're on holiday."

"Yes," she said a trifle coldly and not at all as if she believed what she was saying. "Yes, it is funny." And then directly to Paul, with her wide smile, "What about you? Do you live here? I wish I did."

"Yes. Yes, I do live here," Paul said. "Lived in Walberswick all my life. Are you pleased?"

"Of course I'm delighted. I want your help. Can you tell me whether a boat called *Sea Witch* has come in here during the last two days? I asked at the harbour over there on the other side, but they said *Sea Witch* would be more likely to tie up here because the owner lives in Walberswick."

"So she would," Paul replied. "Why do you want to know about her? Do you want to see the owner?"

"Yes. Urgently. I've got an important message for him."

"The owner is my father," Paul said quietly. "You can give me the message. But who are you? I've never seen you before. Do you know my father?"

David, watching her carefully while Paul was speaking, realized why Mrs Miller had not liked her. There was a cold gleam in her eye when Paul confessed who he was, and he saw how quickly this changed to an eager, excited smile.

"Oh, no. I don't actually *know* your father, but what fun meeting *you*. You mustn't be angry and upset but I promised that I wouldn't give this message to anybody but Mr Channing himself. It's from somebody who knows him well, and as I was coming over here for the day I promised to see him if I could. You live at Heron's Lodge, don't you? I've been there but there was nobody at home. And haven't you got a sister?"

"This is fun, isn't it?" David put in sarcastically. "My name is David Morton—friend of Paul's. May we ask who you are?"

She had a tinkling sort of laugh and directed it now at Paul. It was obvious that she did not care for David.

"My name doesn't really matter. My friends call me Molly, so you can call me that, Paul . . . Are you expecting your father today? He has been out in *Sea Witch*, hasn't he? . . . . Don't be silly, Paul. There's no reason why you shouldn't tell me, is there? I do so want to deliver this message to him personally. A promise is a promise, isn't it?"

"Yes, of course, but I don't know exactly when my father will be back, and if you won't give me the message, the best thing for you to do is to give me your full name and where you're staying and then we'll telephone you when he's back. That will be the best thing, won't it? There's no need for you to hang about here."

This suggestion seemed to surprise her as much as it pleased David. Her gay little laugh tinkled out again but instead of answering the question she asked one.

"You have got a younger sister, haven't you, Paul? Somebody told me that she went off early on the bus this morning with your young friends. Where have they gone?"

Paul realized at last that he had probably said too much. All his old doubts, fears, and suspicions came flooding back and, as he stared at her pretty face while trying to think of an answer to her question, he realized that David was climbing into their dinghy and trying with clumsy fingers to loosen the painter.

"Just realized the time, Paul. We must get across now. You'd never forgive yourself if you were late for this special appointment in Southwold, would you? Nothing to do with me, of course, but if I were you I should resent all these questions about my father . . . Anyway they won't mean so much soon, will they. *Get in, Paul.* You'd better take the oars in this tide. Too strong for me . . . Cheerio, Molly."

For a moment Paul showed his astonishment and nearly asked more about their urgent appointment. Then he saw

David's set face below him in the boat as he struggled with the oars and the current swung the dinghy against the supports of the little pier. Then he jumped into the boat as Molly grabbed for his hand, missed and nearly fell into the swirling water.

"Wait for me!" she shouted. "I want to go to Southwold."

By now David, with one oar, was struggling frantically to push the dinghy away from the pier. The tide was on the turn but the water was very rough and the little boat was soon out of control.

"Give me the oars!" Paul yelled. "Get her away from this pier. *Give me the oars.*"

David slipped back off the seat and passed the oars to Paul. Then he looked up at Molly and when he saw the fury on her face he knew that his suspicions were correct.

"Sorry!" He shouted as Paul controlled the dinghy and edged her away from the wooden piles of the landing stage. "Sorry, Molly! We can't pick you up now. Too rough. We'll send the ferry over. Sorry and all that but we're in a hurry."

"What was all that in aid of, you idiot," Paul gasped as he strained at the oars. "Lucky you chose this dinghy as it happens to be ours. What's all this about an appointment and why couldn't we give her a lift?"

"She's spying on us and I'm sure she wants to spy on your father. She's mixed up in this rotten business, Paul, and she thought she could get round you, and so she would have done if I hadn't been here, you poor boob. Can't you see that we're not the only ones who want to know when and where your father is coming back? Somebody wants him quickly and I suddenly had a brainwave and I think it worked . . . Do you want any help?"

Paul, now scarlet in the face with his efforts to keep the dinghy from being swept out to sea, grunted, "Of course I want help, you idiot. You nearly wrecked us just now so I'm sure we'll be safer if I struggle alone . . . Tell me about your brainwave."

They were in the middle of the river now, with Paul

struggling well against the current so that after a few more strokes they would be carried down with the tide to the ferry landing stage on the Southwold shore.

Meanwhile David went on,

"I thought I'd try to make her believe that we were going to meet your father in Southwold this afternoon, and I'm sure she fell for it. I believe that she dare not let us out of her sight now. Soon as we get over we can hide somewhere and then follow her. I've an idea that she can lead us somewhere very interesting. I don't like what's going on, Paul, and I'm glad now that those kids are out of the way at Orford."

"We're coming in now," Paul gasped. "Grab the ferry boat or one of those posts. I'm checking her all I can."

Paul was skilful on the water and brought his dinghy in very well and two minutes later they were ashore. Then they looked back and saw Molly still waving excitedly on the opposite landing stage.

"Maybe it's as well that we can't hear what she's saying," Paul grinned. "I think you're right about her, David. I know where we can hide, but if she goes straight to South-wold along Ferry Road it will be difficult to keep out of sight. Anyway, let's see what happens."

The two boys waved cheerfully and then climbed up the shingly slope to the rough track leading in one direction to the harbour and the Sailing Club, and to their right to the beach, the sea, and the mouth of the river.

Sitting out of the wind just inside a tarred wooden hut was the ferryman. He nodded gloomily at Paul.

"Hello, Harry," Paul said. "There's a girl over the other side getting hysterical. You'll have to fetch her but don't hurry too much. She's after my friend here."

The man gave not even a flicker of a smile and as they moved away David said, "That's fine, but I hope he's not too long else we shall get cold hanging about. I suppose we've got ten minutes before she gets over the river?"

There is no place in Britain quite like Southwold, and there is no better view of it than from where the boys were hurrying down to Ferry Road which stopped by a caravan camp, two cafés, and a little general store. The town itself was a mile away to the north—on their left—a jumble of red roofs and grey flint walls, towering above which was a great lighthouse as white as alabaster. Farther inland, a mighty church, almost as big as a cathedral, dominated all else. Between the river and the town on its little hill was a great stretch of flat pasture intersected by dykes and dotted with cattle. A narrow road ran inland, weather-beaten for about half a mile to an old farmhouse of grey stone.

When the boys had bought some sandwiches from the café they dodged past some empty caravans and climbed the bank so that they were looking down on to the beach and where the river ran out to the sea. The wind was roaring down from the north, and the sea tumbled on the sand, swirling hungrily against the timbers at the entrance to the harbour, and meeting the muddy waters of the river in such a frenzy of frustration that Paul turned to his friend and said. "No little boat could live in that. It's worse than I thought down here and it will be worse still for the next one or two flood tides. If we lie on the top of the dune here Molly will never see us when she comes down the road. I wonder what she'll do?"

They had not long to wait. They were too far off to see her face but she walked as if she was furious. As soon as she was round the corner into Ferry Road and so out of sight, they ran down to the shelter of the caravans again and moved forward cautiously.

After all it was not so very difficult to follow her without being seen if they kept just below the crest of the bank between the beach and the road. It was hard going through the loose sand and shingle as the wind was in their faces, and twice they flopped down when Molly turned round. But she only looked back along the straight road to the caravan camp, although she also stopped once as if trying to make up her mind where the narrower road turned off at right angles across the marsh to the grey farmhouse.

"That's a lonely house," David whispered. "Rum sort of place to build it. Molly isn't going visiting, is she?"

"Shouldn't think so. It's called Yoxleys and belongs to two old ladies. I've never been there but I believe Father knows them. I'm as curious about this girl now as you are, David. Doesn't fit in here, does she?"

The boys got up and walked on again behind the shelter of the dunes, and David was just remarking that the marsh beyond the road must be at least six feet below the level of the sea when something unforeseen happened. The driver of a car coming from the harbour on the way to Southwold saw Molly struggling against the wind, stopped and offered her a lift. She looked back once along the road and then gratefully got into the car.

"That's done it," Paul said. "And there's not another car in sight, so we shall have to walk the rest. Wait until she's out of sight and then we can get on the road. We'll be lucky if we find her in Southwold now that she's got such a start."

"Remember that she's almost certainly looking for us, and I hope she believes that we're meeting your father," David answered. "We might as well spend the rest of the afternoon dodging each other. You just show me Southwold, Paul."

It was while they were looking around the magnificent old church that David saw Molly again.

"Molly!" he whispered as he pulled Paul back behind one of the great pillars.

"Let's get outside and watch her for a change," Paul suggested. "If she's meeting anyone else we'll follow her, and if she's still searching for us she'll soon be out and it will be interesting to know where she looks next."

They slipped away without being seen and hid behind a tomb in the churchyard. When Molly came out of the church alone, they followed her into the street and watched her as she looked into several antique shops and an attractive little book shop in the High Street. While she was in the latter, David suggested that they should lay a trap for her.

"Let her see us when she comes out but of course we shan't notice her. We'll go into that café opposite, choose a table for three or four and if she is really still after us she'll come in too. We'll pretend that we want to get rid of her because we're expecting somebody important—your father, actually. See what I mean?"

Paul laughed. "Yes. We're to be nervous and on edge and trying to get rid of her all the time, and the more we fuss the more she'll want to stay with us. Of course. This could be amusing. She'll have to show her hand sooner or later."

They crossed the street and looked in a shop window. As soon as they saw Molly's reflection they went into the café and sat down. They were exchanging anxious whispers when she came in and they both managed to look amazed and embarrassed when she stopped by their table.

"I never expected to see you two rude boys again," she said brightly. "Nobody has ever left me standing on a landing stage before. But just to show you that you're forgiven you can give me some tea." And, as they had hoped, she chose a chair between them and sat down.

"Sorry about that, Molly," David mumbled. "Didn't mean to be rude but we were in a hurry . . . Nice to see you again but we were just saying we didn't like this place much, weren't we, Paul?"

"Yes, that's what we were saying. Actually we were just going to try somewhere else, but you stay of course."

"Nonsense," Molly said. "We'll all stay and have tea together. I suppose you've met your friend by now? You *were* in a hurry, weren't you! Is everything all right now?"

The boys put on a very good act. They were so nervous and unhappy and looked so often at the door that Molly got jumpy, too, and eventually snapped, "For goodness sake stop fidgeting! What is the matter with you? If you're waiting for somebody why don't you say so? Are you expecting your father, Paul?"

Paul dropped a slice of cake on the floor in his agitation.

"I didn't say so, did I? Anyway, it's time we went, David. You pay the bill and we'll go. Molly will excuse us, I know."

"I'll do nothing of the sort. You're very ungallant, but if you're going to walk back to the ferry I'll come with you."

David gave Paul a wink as he paid the bill. There was no doubt now that Molly had swallowed the bait and was determined to discover what they had been doing.

As they walked back together along Ferry Road, she asked again when Paul was expecting his father.

"You will remember that I have a special message for him, won't you? Were you waiting for him in Southwold?"

"We've done all we wanted to do in Southwold, thanks," David said shortly. "Why don't you give Paul this mysterious message and be done with it?"

Molly was now almost as short of temper as she was of breath. She was not very tall and the boys walked fast with long strides. She decided not to answer his last question.

Every vestige of summer had now fled. The wind roared over the bank which kept the sea back from Ferry Road and they could hear the waves thundering on the beach. They had just passed the turning of the narrow road which led across the marsh to Yoxleys when she looked back over her shoulder and stopped without explanation. The boys turned too, and were just in time to see a large black car swing out of Ferry Road up towards the old house.

David turned to Molly and realized that she was genuinely surprised—almost shocked—at something she had just seen.

"Friends of yours, Molly?" David asked, and she turned on him in a fury.

"Don't be a fool. How should I know who they are? Are you two crossing in your dinghy? Isn't it too rough?"

"We'll go and see," Paul said. "You coming too? I doubt if I can row three over."

"I'll see what I'll do when we get there," she said.

The tide was low and the muddy water not too rough as Paul leaned over the landing stage and untied the painter.

"Jump in, David," he said. "I'll cope. Are you going to give me that message for my father, Molly?"

"I can't. I've told you I can't, but if you'll tell me when

he'll be home I'll come over right away to see him . . . I'm going back to Southwold now."

"How can we find you then, Molly?" David asked. "Where did you say you were staying?"

"I didn't say, David. I'll be seeing you again. Good-bye."

Paul pushed off.

"The girl's crazy," he grunted. "After hanging on best part of the afternoon she now wants to get rid of us."

"True enough," David agreed. "She changed her mind after seeing that car. I haven't got the nerve to ask you to row back again, Paul, and I've just remembered Rose and the twins; but I'd like to know where Molly's going now."

He raised his hand as she waved and hurried back towards the road by the caravan camp. The boys would have been surprised if they had seen her turn, ten minutes later, down the narrow road which led only to Yoxleys where a sleek black car was now standing in the yard.

But neither David nor Paul had time to think about her for, after mooring the dinghy on the Walberswick shore, they saw Rose, the twins and Macbeth running towards them from the Millers' cottage.

Rose reached them first. She had been crying.

"Why didn't you leave a message? How do you think we knew where you were? Only just now Mrs Miller told us that you rowed over hours ago after talking to a red-headed girl. We've been phoning and phoning home for hours."

Then Dickie broke in, "You may like to know that *Sea Witch* is back at Orford, Mr Channing was on it and has been to a place called Zutten because of a clue we found ——"

"Where's Father now?" Paul shouted. "Where is he?"

There was a pause before Rose gulped back a sob and said, "We don't know but we think he drove off in a big black car from the *Harbour Lights* with the man who was in the bar there the other day. We saw the car drive off but didn't actually see the driver or Daddy. You see, we had to escape because a chauffeur who fell off *Sea Witch* into the water was after us——"

"You're *all* crazy," David said. "What's all this about a chauffeur?" But before any of them could answer, a low green car roared down the road towards them and pulled up with a squeal of brakes.

"Hello, you lot," James Wilson smiled. "Any news?"

9. Yoxleys

Richard channing was dragged from the deep sleep of exhaustion in bedroom Number Three at *Harbour Lights* by the sound of a familiar voice. He did not want to wake. Nothing, at this moment of his life, was as important as sleep.

"Wake up, my dear Channing. Wake up!"

He turned resentfully and buried his face in the pillow, but the voice hunted him down and hard fingers grasped his shoulder and shook him reluctantly awake.

"Come along, Channing. I have news for you. *Wake up!*"

He looked up to see Simon Donald standing over him. And with recognition, the memory of how this man had fooled him came rushing back, and Channing flushed with anger as he sat up and shook his shoulder free.

"How did you get here and what do you want?" he snapped as he swung his feet off the bed. "Why can't you leave me alone?"

"Leave you alone, my dear fellow? Why should I wish to do that? Although you didn't tell me at the time, I assumed that you would return to Orford as soon as your mission was completed and I decided to come and meet you. Have you been successful, Channing? You have been so quick that I feel sure I can congratulate you. I should like you to tell me all about it and then, of course, when you have handed over the receipt for the charts, there is some finance to settle . . ."

As Channing watched his enemy he was sure that something was amiss. Donald's face and eyes told him nothing, but they never had, and in that moment he realized that they never would. He was cold and calculating and Channing decided that, with a little patience, he might discover more about this evil man. It would be wise to let him do the talking for a while. Although, above all else, he now wanted to get away once and for all from Donald and his temptations of easy money, the break must be such that Rose and Paul would never, never know what had been going on. And as he thought of his deception of his two children, he knew for certain that he must make no mistake now.

"Don't worry, Donald," he yawned. "I've got the receipt, but I'd rather sleep now than take the money unless you've got it in your pocket. I don't know how you got in here but you can get out as soon as you like. I want some more sleep."

Donald's features relaxed.

"It was because I was so sure that you would be successful, and because I realized how tired you would be, that I came here today on the chance of meeting you, my dear fellow. I think you deserve more comfort than this inn can offer you, Channing, and that is why I woke you."

"What's that got to do with it? This place is good enough for me until I get home. I've known it for years and it suits me, and I don't believe you came in here just to welcome me home. Here's the receipt, but you'll read it from that side of the bed, if you please, and I'll hang on to it until you pass over the money. You've brought it, I suppose?"

He took his wallet from his pocket and produced the scrap of paper signed by Andrea about twenty-four hours ago. He was surprised that Donald barely glanced at it, and even more surprised when he said,

"I knew I could rely on you, Channing. I have enjoyed our business contacts and hope this won't be the last. The truth is that I was passing this way, and hoping that you might be back, called in here to ask if you had been seen. No doubt you'll be surprised to know that I'm to be a fairly close neighbour of yours for I've taken a house in your district. I'd like to show it to you and ask your advice about some matters. My car is here so we can start at once and we can settle our business there . . . Keep the receipt, my dear fellow, until we can settle up. I really am delighted that you were able to deliver those charts with comparatively so little trouble."

"There was plenty of trouble coming back," Channing said, as he tried to work out the information he had just been given. What possible reason could Donald have for taking a house in the Southwold district? Then he remembered that John Jackson had lived and worked at Southwold, and that the most famous of his pictures was "The Red Mill" which had been stolen, presumably by Donald, and which he himself had just carried to the unpleasant Andrea in Zutten. Perhaps Donald was on the trail of more J.J. pictures? Channing then remembered the article in the *Clarion* on this subject, and realized how deeply he was concerned in this wretched business. It would perhaps be wiser to go with Donald now and find out where he was living and what he was up to. He was determined not to take any money for this last trip now that he knew what he had been doing, but before he finally broke free he must be certain that Paul and Rose would never find out what part he had been playing.

"I had plenty of trouble coming back," he repeated. "I was single-handed, tired, and there's bad weather on the way. I want to go home and finish my sleep, but if you've got your car and are going my way I'll be glad of a lift."

"I think we'll get back to my place first, if you don't mind. This has all turned out splendidly and I'm much looking forward to showing you my little place. No need now to settle up with Hawkins. I'll do that when I next see him. Let's go at once!"

Channing pulled a jersey over his head, put on his jacket and followed Donald out of the room.

Donald waited for a moment at the top of the stairs, but there was no sound from below.

"Quickly and quietly, Channing," he whispered urgently. "Follow me without question, please. I do not want either of us to give anybody any explanations just now. You can come back tomorrow."

Channing was at once suspicious. Why all the secrecy?

But he said nothing and followed Donald out through the back of the inn into the yard. He had seen the big black Wolseley before but he had never ridden in it. It was extremely comfortable, but before he had settled down next to the driving seat they had swung out into the road and were accelerating fast. If he had looked into the mirror, he would have seen Rose, the twins, and Macbeth running round the bend in the road on the way from the harbour. But he did not, and long afterwards he confessed that he never knew whether Donald had seen them either.

What he was sure of, however, was that Donald drove fast and recklessly. Never before had he seen him so excitable, but it was not until they passed the Walberswick turning that Donald said, "You will be glad to be home and united with your family. I have never seen Heron's Lodge, but now that I am living so close to you I must call and see you soon. I should like to meet your family, Channing. That would indeed be a pleasure."

Channing made no answer to the suggestion that Donald should meet his family. There was no doubting the threat behind his words, and perhaps for the first time Channing fully realized the danger of this man sitting beside him.

They were on the main road now, running north through the village of Blythburgh which once had been a great port. On their left, crowning a little hill, was the magnificent church, and soon they crossed the river Blyth which ran out to the sea between Southwold and Walberswick about five miles away.

Turning right they saw the church tower and white lighthouse of Southwold showing clearly against the skyline, and Channing was wondering whether he had been a fool to leave Orford so hurriedly, when he realized that they had turned into Ferry Road.

"Perhaps you know the little house I have taken," Donald said suddenly. "We turn off here to the right."

"So you've taken Yoxleys? I've been in the house several times," Channing replied. "I think it would be as well to get our business talk over-as soon as possible, Donald. I don't like the look of the weather and I want to get home."

Donald smiled grimly without reply, while Channing wondered what possible reason his enemy could have for taking such an isolated, inconvenient old farmhouse. What game was he playing? Ferry Road was deserted but for three young people walking ahead of them towards the harbour about one hundred yards past the turning. As Donald braked to turn sharply to the right and the car swung round towards Yoxleys, the young woman turned quickly at the sound of the car. Channing idly noted that she was red-haired and that the back view of one of the two young men with her reminded him vaguely of Paul.

The outhouses and barns of Yoxleys were shabby and neglected, but Channing had little time to look around him when his companion drove into the yard.

"Welcome to Yoxleys, my dear fellow," Donald said as he grasped Channing's arm, led him into the porch and unlocked the front door. "A cup of tea will be welcome. Come in here and I will order it."

Channing remembered the sitting-room, which was not unlike his own at Heron's Lodge—long and low, but with windows facing south across the marsh towards the river and french windows opening on to the garden at the side of the house. He knew that the two old sisters who owned Yoxleys were always ready to rent it furnished and, as they were poor, a let to somebody with money, like Donald, in mid-September would mean much to them both. Although Donald was a crook, he certainly was not a fake picture dealer, and Channing was surprised that he could live in a house so cluttered up with useless furniture and knick-knacks.

As Channing dodged round one of the tables on his way to the window, he heard Donald's voice in the hall and wondered who he had got to work for him in such an isolated house. Then he came back, invited Channing to sit down near the smoking fire and switched on one of the lamps. He then crossed to the french windows, tried them to see if they were locked and drew the curtains across them.

"Cosy little place this," he said as he stood with his back to the fire and looked down on Channing, who was not feeling at all comfortable. "The woman is bringing tea but we can start our business. Kindly pass over the receipt now, Channing, and I will see that your return fare to Zutten is paid."

Before he could answer they were interrupted by a thump on the door and a big, untidy-looking woman came in with a tea-tray.

"Put in on this table, Mrs Holmes," Donald ordered and as Channing looked up he heard the woman draw in her breath sharply in surprise.

He knew her. Emma Holmes, a widow from Walberswick. A rather stupid, weak woman but vaguely good-hearted, and as he met her eyes he saw not only recognition but astonishment—and almost fear. He was not to know that Emma was already regretting taking this job, but he realized that it would be better if Donald did not know that they knew each other. It was stupid of him to have employed a local woman.

Channing turned in his chair so that Donald could not see his face and, raising a finger to his lips, shook his head slightly, praying that Emma would understand. She did, but her hand was shaking so badly that the cups rattled as she put the tray on the table. Channing glanced away casually, but Donald was looking at him with sudden suspicion and when the door had closed behind Emma, "I'm expecting some friends—perhaps it would be more suitable to refer to them as colleagues," he said. "I've been thinking that as you are now here, safe and sound at Yoxleys, it might be better for you to stay the night."

Even as he was speaking, Channing heard the sound of a car arriving and then the slam of the doors.

"Ah! A little sooner than I thought. This will be a very pleasant meeting. Pour yourself a cup of tea Channing, and remain where you are."

He crossed the room and was out of the door before Channing could rise. As he got up he heard the click of the lock as the key was turned from the other side. He was locked in; Donald must be far more suspicious of him than he had suspected. Perhaps he had been fooling him all the time?

He knelt down with his ear to the keyhole and heard the deep rough voice of a man say, "I've got the J.J. from Derbyshire, guv'nor, but it's going to cost you a lot. Wasn't far from trouble on this job and I've got to lay low."

"Nice work, Brown," came Donald's quieter voice. "You can give me a full report shortly and hand over the picture . . . I see you've picked up Molly. I have an idea that you have been wasting your time, my dear. We have an important visitor in there. I'm sure you will be interested to meet him . . . Yes, Molly. Mr Channing is enjoying a cup of tea in there, but we have to make sure that he does not leave us . . ."

Channing needed to hear no more. He had been a simpleton and was now trapped. He got up stiffly from his knees, at last positive that he must escape from Yoxleys at once. The french windows would probably be easiest, but as he turned and ran towards them, he blundered into one of the little tables. As he stumbled forward he clutched at the standard lamp and brought it crashing to the floor. The bulb smashed as he fell and, as he picked himself up, the door behind him opened and he saw an enormous man rushing at him with Donald just behind.

He had about a two yards start and flung himself in despair at the curtained french windows. They burst open under his weight with a crash and tinkle of breaking glass, but he tripped over the sill and fell heavily on to the paving stones outside. For a moment he lay there, more than half stunned, and from far, far away heard Donald's hateful voice saying,

"He knows too much and is trying to run away. Dear, dear! How noisy and tiresome of Mr Channing. Make sure that he stays with us as a guest, Mr Brown."

Like a beaten boxer Channing tried to stand up and escape to freedom, but he was so weak and dizzy that he hardly felt the force of the big man's fist as it cracked against his jaw.

10. Night at Heron's Lodge

WHEN THE SUN went down on that same September evening the wind died with it. Darkness came soon and although the moon was nearly full she showed only a hint of her pale radiance behind the clouds. Without the sound of the wind, the boom of the breakers on the flat beaches of East Anglia became more obvious and fishermen all down the coast, suspicious of the lull, helped each other to drag their boats up beyond the steep ridges of shingle left by the high tides. All up the coasts from Scotland to the Thames estuary anxious men were watching the sea, ready to warn the authorities and the police of danger.

In Heron's Lodge, David, Paul, Rose and the twins finished their supper and tried to pretend that they were not all on edge waiting for the telephone to ring or for Richard Channing to come home. James Wilson had come back with them and they had told him their respective stories. He had listened in silence, asked a few questions and then gone off in his car after promising to telephone them with any news.

But there was no telephone call and James had still not returned when they all went to bed.

Mary was sharing Rose's room on the first floor while Dickie and David were together across the landing. Paul's room was under the roof on the top floor. The two girls were tired and did not say much as they undressed. Soon after the light was out Mary sat up suddenly and said, "I want Mackie, Rose. I know he isn't supposed to sleep on beds but I want him tonight. The wind is blowing hard again and I'm sure Mackie is lonely in the kitchen."

"But he always sleeps in the kitchen by the stove, Mary. Why do you want him specially tonight?"

As Mary scrambled into her dressing-gown she said,
"I didn't think you'd ask me to explain *why* I want him,
Rose, I just know that I do and I'm sure he wants me . . ."

The landing light was on, and as Mary ran down
the stairs she saw Macbeth on the mat outside the sitting-
room door with his head on one side. He turned at the sound
of her soft whistle from the stair and bounded up to her. A
minute later Mary was back in bed and Mackie curled up
under the eiderdown at her feet.

"Sorry I was silly about him, Mary," Rose said. "I like
him here too. I'm tired now so God bless."

But Rose could not sleep. The wind was coming up with
the tide again. The window began to rattle and she wondered whether to get out and try to wedge it with a wad of
paper. But it always did rattle and she was warm and comfortable in bed. She snuggled her head into the pillow,
closed her eyes tight and tried to forget that still she did not
know where her father was. It would not matter if only he
would let them know. Rose buried her face in the pillow
as the tears pricked her eyes. She loved her father so very
much.

Soon after, she slept uneasily while the old house creaked
and the rattling windows were misted with the salt spray
carried inland by the wind. There were other sounds too—
the sound, for instance, of a car and the slamming of a door
and a step in the hall below at which Macbeth lifted his
head and growled. Perhaps it was one of these noises which
gave Rose the nightmare which wakened her from her
uneasy sleep.

Suddenly, almost more real than reality itself, she was
alone at the end of a long, brightly-lighted corridor. The
wall on her left was bare—no doors, no windows and no
pictures, and painted a hard, gleaming blue. Along the
opposite wall stretched an infinity of closed doors getting
smaller and smaller and smaller as far as she could see. All
these doors were white and the wall between was red, and
she knew that behind one of these doors she was to find her
father. This was something she had to do. He was waiting

for her. He wanted her. Not Paul, nor David, nor the twins, but Rose. She was sure he was in great danger, and before she began to search for him she remembered that twice already during the last few days she had opened a bedroom door hoping to find him, and been faced only with an empty, tumbled bed. Here, in this long corridor, was where he had been all the time. No wonder they had not heard from him. No wonder they had not known where to look. She was probably now in the house of the man with the big black car—the man in whom James Wilson was interested—and her father was waiting for her in one of these rooms.

She stepped forward and opened the first door. The room was empty and unfurnished—not even a tumbled bed. She tried the next. The same, except that the room was smaller and the window bigger. The next and the next and the next were the same, only each room was smaller than the last and the windows larger and closer to the door. And yet she was still sure that her father was near and was waiting for her, but if the rooms got much smaller there would soon be no room for him. And then, with her fingers on the handle of the next door, she paused. This was the room, she was sure. This must be the one, and though something warned her that if she opened this door there would be no floor but just a space beyond the door, she was still certain that her father needed her and was waiting for her to come to him.

She turned the handle but the door was locked. She struggled, screamed—and woke.

"Rose, Rose! Wake up, Rose! What's happened?"

It was Mary's voice, and with a sense of glorious relief Rose realized that she was in her own bed at home. She sat up with the tears still wet on her face and switched on the bed-side light.

Mary was sitting up, too, and clutching Macbeth.

"What is it, Rose? You were crying and calling out. Was it a horrid dream?"

"I'm sorry, Mary. Really I am. I s'pose I woke you up. It was a nightmare about my father. He wants me, Mary. I know he does. I know that he's in trouble. I was afraid before, because I didn't know, but now I'm sure that something awful has happened . . . *I don't know what to do, Mary,*" and with that she switched out the light and slipped under the bed-clothes again.

For half a minute Mary, sitting up in bed, said nothing. Macbeth's rough coat was against her face and twice he turned to lick her cheek. She knew that Rose was frightened, but she was also sure that it would be silly and wrong to upset her by pretending that she was not scared! To her distress Mary then realized that her friend was trying to stifle sobs.

"A nightmare is never as bad when you wake up, Rose," she whispered. "You're awake now. Do you know what my twin calls a nightmare. A night horse. Isn't he silly? Don't cry any more, Rose. I hate it. Talk to me until you go to sleep again."

Before Rose could answer, Macbeth growled, gave his warning bark and then jumped off Mary's bed.

"Quiet, Mackie!" Mary hissed and then, hearing the scratch of his claws on the door, she realized that the wind had died down again and that the house was comparatively quiet.

"Mackie can hear something," she whispered.

They strained their ears but there was only the thudding of their own hearts and Macbeth's soft growl.

"Perhaps Daddy has come home?" Rose whispered. "Shall we go down and see?"

"You stay here and I'll go and wake my brothers," Mary replied. "On the way I'll listen at the top of the stairs . . . No, Rose. I'm not scared really. I'll leave the door open and I'll know you're here, but we must tell the boys before one of us goes down. I'll take Mackie with me else he'll make a noise."

"You're very brave, Mary, and if you'll come with me I'd like us to go down together to see whether my father is there . . . Or perhaps he's already in his room?" And then, at the thought of once again opening a door to see if he had come home, she covered her face with her hands.

Mary clenched her teeth to stop them from chattering, got out of bed, slipped on her dressing-gown and with one hand on Macbeth's collar opened the door.

The landing and the stairs were in darkness and she stood for a moment in a pool of yellow light from the room behind her. She stood quite still with Macbeth quivering at her side. Another gust of wind rattled the windows while the floor-boards creaked in sympathy. Upstairs the door of Paul's big room was fidgeting and from the hall she heard the steady ticking of the grandfather clock.

Thud. Thud. Thud went Mary's heart. Her brother's room was only a few paces away but, just for a moment, she could not find the courage to cross the landing. Then the wind died down and in the sudden quiet she heard the murmur of a man's voice from somewhere below. The hair bristled on Mackie's back and he growled again.

Mary turned and waved to Rose who was sitting up in bed, then ran across the landing and was in the boys' room, with Macbeth at her heels, in a few seconds. She stood with her back to the door and switched on the light.

Both boys were asleep and neither stirred. Macbeth ran across the room, took a flying leap on to Dickie's bed and began to lick his face while Mary shook David's shoulder till he yawned and turned over.

"Warisit? Go away. It's too late," he growled and then, seeing his sister's anxious face within a few inches of his own, he sat up and said, "What's wrong, Mary?"

"Oh, David! Rose had a nightmare and is in a terrible fuss about her father, an' Mackie knows there's something wrong and I've just heard men talking downstairs. Rose wonders whether Mr Channing has come home but she doesn't dare to go down by herself to see."

David groped under the pillow for his watch.

"It's just on one o'clock. Wake Dickie properly so that he doesn't shout the house down and keep as quiet as you can. I'll go down and see what's happening. It's probably James Wilson. He said he might come back very late and we told him he could sleep in Mr Channing's room . . . You're shivering, Mary. Not really scared, are you? Take Dickie with you and go back to Rose. I'll go downstairs. Up the Lone Piners!"

"Up the Lone Piners!" Dickie echoed from the next bed. "I don't know what this is about, but if my twin has discovered a dastardly plot or something then I'm on her side."

Dickie crept away with his twin and Macbeth and David followed after putting on some warmer clothes. He stood at the top of the stairs and listened and was soon convinced that somebody was talking in the sitting-room.

Next he tried the door of Mr Channing's room and it opened at once. Nobody there and no sign of James either. Surely Channing had not come home with a friend at this time in the morning without announcing himself? Perhaps though, just because it was so late, he had decided not to disturb them?

David was baffled and unhappy about the mysterious disappearance of Mr Channing. Before going to bed he had once again talked it all over with Paul and persuaded him to go to the police if there was no news in the morning. After a few moments, consideration he returned to Rose's room where the twins and Mackie were sitting on her bed.

"Is it my father, David? Have you been down? Mary says there are two men there."

He shook his head. "I don't know. I haven't been down yet but I don't think it's your father, Rose, although I'm sure we're going to have news of him soon. Listen all of you and do as I say. I'm going down now to see what's happening but I want Rose to go up and wake Paul. Tell him quickly what's happened and that I'm waiting for him in the hall. You others can wait here or on the landing. Don't come down until I tell you, and Mary must keep Mackie quiet. Off you go, Rose. Get Paul down as quickly as you can."

So David, looking braver than he felt, crept down the stairs into the dark hall. The wind had died away again and Heron's Lodge was fairly quiet—silent enough, except for the odd creaks and groans of any old house, for David to hear the click of the door of Paul's room on the top landing. And quiet enough also for him to hear the tick of the grandfather clock, and the unmistakable murmur of a man's voice behind the closed door of the sitting-room under which a thin gleam of light was showing.

David knelt down and put his ear to the keyhole. The wind was whistling into the hall under the front door and his teeth began to chatter. He could not be sure, but the voice sounded like Wilson's and suddenly he realized that he had not got a companion but was speaking on the telephone.

He thought he heard "Good-bye" and then the faint "ting" of the bell as the receiver was replaced. David got up from his knees and backed away in case Wilson was now going to bed. He looked back and saw Paul coming carefully downstairs and the others staring at them from the landing. As Paul stepped into the hall David whispered.

"I believe it's Wilson on the telephone. Shall we go and see what he's doing? After all, it's your house."

Paul nodded, but when he touched the handle they heard the voice ask for another number. "Sounded like Whitehall something or other," David whispered, and Paul replied, "The telephone is out of sight of the door, you remember. I'm going to open it a crack and hold it so that we can make sure. We *must* be sure, David. It might be my father."

David nodded and then felt a cold hand slip into his own which was in his dressing-gown pocket.

"It's us," Rose breathed. "Don't be cross, David. We had to come. We heard what Paul said. *Open the door, Paul.* It's got to be Daddy."

Suddenly the voice was clear. It *was* James Wilson.

"Scotland Yard? Good. 262, please. That you, Bill? This is James Wilson of the *Clarion*, speaking from Walberswick . . . Yes, that's it. WALBERSWICK. Next door to Southwold and I can't shout because I don't want to wake the house . . . Now listen, Bill, because this is something . . . Yes, of course, I'm on the job for the paper, but I've just been to my editor and he says it's O.K. to put you wise now. It's the J.J. picture-stealing business I'm working on. It's time you chaps got on to this and you'd better come up here at once. There's really something doing . . . Of course I'm serious. Would I ring you up at two o'clock in the morning if I wasn't? . . . Now listen. Simon Donald, the picture dealer—yes, of course you know the man. I know you do because I was asking questions about him the other day. Simon Donald has been seen about up here and somehow the Suffolk coast isn't quite like him! I suppose you know that John Jackson the artist lived in Southwold and nearly all his pictures were painted in this district? Anyway Donald is about and there's something very odd going on with a man called Channing who's disappeared from his house here after a one-man sailing trip in his own boat in the North Sea. I'm sure this Channing knows Donald and has got something to do with——"

But he said no more, for suddenly Rose pushed past Paul and David, crashed back the door and ran into the room sobbing with rage. She flung herself at the startled Wilson and pummelled him with her fists.

"You liar! You wicked liar!" she cried. "How *dare* you accuse my father like that . . . We thought you were our friend and you're nothing but a liar . . . Don't let him do it, David. Stop him!"

But for once Paul was before David. He snatched the telephone from Wilson and pulling with both hands tore the cable out of the wall.

Rose, now crying on the sofa, had never seen her brother so angry and had never been so proud of him. Mary ran over to comfort her while Dickie dropped Macbeth who began to bark. David began to speak but thought better of it as Paul, still with the snapped telephone wires in his hand, faced Wilson.

"Get out of here, Wilson. Rose was right. We thought you were our friend. You've come into my father's house as a friend and if he was here he'd kick you out. Just get out quickly . . . *Get out and never come back!*"

Wilson licked his dry lips and looked round. Three boys and two girls. School kids! He tried to speak but for a moment no words came. He looked round at them but none of them would meet his eyes. Then, "David?" he whispered. "You understand?"

David shook his head.

Wilson moved to the sofa and clumsily but tenderly touched Rose's hair.

She shook her head free and looked away as Wilson, in a silence that could be felt, stepped slowly across the room and went out through the open door into the hall.

A sudden gust of wind moaned round the house and rattled the windows as Paul, with misery in his eyes, dropped the telephone cable and walked over to close the door.

Rose stood up and as David put out a hand to help her she flung her arms round him.

"It isn't true about Daddy! We all know it isn't true, don't we? We've got to find him now ourselves—before Wilson or anybody else. Promise you'll all help."

11. The Prisoner

IT WAS NEARLY two hours before Richard Channing
recovered his senses after being knocked down by the big
man in the living-room of Yoxleys and it took him ten
minutes to realize that he was in an old wicker chair which
creaked when he moved. He was very cold, his head and
jaw ached and he felt sick. When he tried to sit up he found
that he was covered with an old rug. There was a curious
smell, too, and after a little he guessed that it must be coal
and that he was a prisoner in a cellar. He opened his eyes
and clenched his teeth to still a cry of pain as he turned his
head to the left. A few feet away, and presumably at the
level of the ceiling, was a greyish rectangle of light which
must be the window, and as he became more used to the
gloom of his prison he realized that it was unglazed and
barred. Then he became aware of the moaning of a great
wind and the distant roar of the sea.

He sat still until his head cleared and memories of the last
few hours came flooding back. He remembered the last
words he had heard before the big man had knocked him
unconscious.

"He knows too much," Donald had said in his quiet,
sinister voice. "He's trying to run away. Dear, dear! How
noisy and tiresome of Mr Channing. Make sure that he
stays with us as a guest, Mr Brown."

Anyway, there was now no doubt that Donald had suspected him and, for the first time, Channing realized that
Andrea in Zutten might well have telephoned his suspicions
to Donald in London or indeed to Yoxleys.

He raised his wrist to see the time but his watch had gone.
He moved himself painfully in the chair and felt in his
pockets. He had not been carrying much of value, but

neither his wallet nor his fountain-pen was there. Then he
got unsteadily to his feet.

For a moment he was so dizzy that he stumbled and a
stab of pain nearly split his head. Then the wave of sickness
passed and he stood upright and fumbled in his pocket for
matches. With shaking fingers he struck one, and as the little
yellow flame spluttered into life he saw that the cellar was
only about twelve feet square. He stepped cautiously towards the window and stumbled and fell over a piece of
coal. When he got to his feet he was shaking with childish
fury at the unkindness of fate. He tried again and realized
that there was a pile of coal under the window and that he
must scramble up it if he wanted to test the strength of the
bars. Very carefully he trod on the coal and brought several
large lumps crashing down about his ankles. He cursed but
persevered and then, by reaching up, he grasped the iron
bars. There were five of these and they were all firm.
Although he tugged and shook with all his strength, not one
of them moved a fraction of an inch. He slid down the pile
of coal again realizing that, foolishly, he had not yet tried
the cellar door; but by now, in the darkness, he had lost his
sense of direction. He struck another match with his back
to the window and saw the door. He stumbled forward to it
and could feel that it was an old-fashioned, solid affair
crossed with iron bands. It was locked from the outside.

Then he sat down again in the chair and tried to consider
calmly what was the best thing to do. If indeed he had been
deserted and was still in Yoxleys, his chances of escape were
slender. Nobody would hear him if he banged on the door
and there was no way of signalling through the barred
window which was apparently at ground level. Even if he
broke up the chair and tried to make a torch from the
lengths of wicker, the chances were that the wind would
blow out the flames. And even if it did not, nobody was
likely to be prowling round Yoxleys at this time of night. As
he knew well, few people came along the lonely road that
led only to the farmhouse and no doubt that was one of the
reasons why Donald had rented it.

Anyway there seemed no sense in staying here in silence.
Get out he must, but if he could not use the door or window
he had better find out whether anyone was in the house. If
his captors were still in Yoxleys they must open the cellar
door some time, and once it had been opened there might
be a chance of escape.

It seemed worth trying to see if anybody was upstairs, so
he picked up a heavy lump of coal and crashed it against
the lock again and again until it split his hands. Then he
put his ear to the door and listened, but could hear nothing.
He tried again with another chunk of coal but had the sense
not to waste his breath shouting. Then as he moved back to
find another lump of coal, he heard the rasp of a key in the
lock and when he looked down he saw a thin line of light
across the floor. Suddenly he wondered if there would be a
chance of escape if he hid behind the door as it opened? The
lock clicked, and as he slipped back behind the opening
door, a hated but familiar voice said quietly, "Just behave
yourself, Channing. There are three of us and you haven't a
chance."

Then the beam of a torch slashed through the darkness
with the door not more than six inches ajar. The light
searched every corner of the cellar and then Donald spoke
again.

"The foolish fellow is behind the door, Brown," and even
as he spoke he pushed the heavy door back with all his
strength.

Channing was not ready for this and the door struck him
on the shoulder so that he stumbled back against the wall as
three men stepped into the cellar. Brown, who was first,
swung his torch round. The beam dazzled Channing as
Brown jumped forward and aimed a blow at him but the
former had the satisfaction of hitting him on the ear and was
delighted to hear his curse of surprise. Then the second man
flung himself at Channing's knees and brought him down in
a rugger tackle amongst the broken coal just inside the door.
Brown hauled him up and flung him back into the chair.

"Don't be a fool, Channing," Donald said testily. "I told

will be yours. Quite an attractive child, your daughter."

Channing listened in amazement. There had been veiled threats before, but never anything quite as brutal as the suggestion that Rose would suffer for her father's mistakes. As his anger rose, he forgot that his children had friends staying with them and thought of them alone, more or less defenceless, at Heron's Lodge. And so he lost his judgment and his temper, and as Donald stopped speaking and felt for his cigarette case, Channing jumped from his chair in an attempt to reach the cold, sneering face of his enemy.

He did not have a chance of course. Smith he could have managed, but the enormous Brown flung him to the ground again. He fought gamely and managed to grasp Donald's ankles and bring him down on to the pile of coal. But a blow on the head from the heavy torch wielded by the cursing Donald sent him down again, and the next thing he realized was that icy cold water was dropping down his face and that once more a cruel beam of light was in his eyes.

"He's O.K., guv'nor," Brown was saying. "And cold clean water is more than he's worth."

Channing lay limp although it was difficult to control his chattering teeth as the cold water trickled down his chest and neck. He realized now that he was bound to the chair.

"Check that rope," Donald snapped. "You'll both be in trouble if he fools us again. No more risks."

Poor Channing was certainly most uncomfortable now. It seemed as if the rope that was binding his ankles was attached in some way to that securing his wrists behind the chair, for the slightest attempted movement of his numbed feet sent a stab of pain through his hands.

"Now, Channing. I know you can hear me. I've wasted too much time with you because I thought you had some common sense and you would prefer to spend the night more comfortably upstairs. Now I have no choice. I doubt if you will sleep well down here but you have chosen to do so. I am a humane man and so you will not be gagged. Nobody will hear you if you care to strain your voice."

He swung the beam of the torch towards the door and

then turned to unlock it. Then he stood aside for Brown and Smith and followed them without another glance at the prisoner who heard the lock click home once again.

It was very dark now and Channing could only just see the position of the barred window. The wind was still roaring outside, and a cold draught soothed his hot face which was throbbing with pain. He tried to relax and think calmly. There seemed no sense in exhausting himself by trying to escape from his bonds, for even if he did so there was no chance of getting out of the cellar until somebody came to see him in the morning. He felt faint and sick with the pain at his wrists and ankles and at the thought of Donald's threats against Paul and Rose. He did not really believe that his enemy could do them much harm, because however desperate he might be it seemed more likely that he and his confederates would leave Southwold tomorrow, possibly taking him with them as a prisoner because they dared not leave him behind. They knew now that he would certainly betray them as soon as he was free. But would he dare to tell the police if Donald took Rose off with him as a hostage? As he thought of this possibility he struggled violently to free himself, but Brown and Smith had done their work only too well.

He lay back exhausted and after a little, while the wind howled outside, he dozed. Although he never knew how long he had lain bound and semi-conscious in the chair, it was in fact nearly four hours later that he was roused by the scraping sound of the key in the lock.

Slowly, inch by inch the door opened and the darkness of the cellar was relieved by the flickering flame of a candle. He turned his head painfully, wondering who his visitor could be this time, but all he could see was a skinny hand holding a cheap enamelled candlestick.

Then, in the draught between window and door, the candle blew out and the darkness surged back again.

"Are you there, sir? What have they done to you? Can you hear me? I'll close the door and light the candle again."

Emma Holmes!

His throat was dry and painful.

"Good for you, Emma!" he croaked. "I'm tied in this chair and can't move. Don't let them hear you. Close the door quietly and lock it from the inside. Light up the candle again if you've got any matches."

He heard the lock click again and then knew that she was fumbling and moving about a few feet away. He heard the unmistakable rattle of a match-box and then the splutter of a match as the candle was lit. She came over to the chair and held the flame high so that they could see each other.

"They're a lot of devils, sir," she whispered hoarsely. "That's what they are. They're a bad, wicked lot and I'm clearing out. I've had enough. Never mind about the good money I says to myself. This is no place for Emma Holmes I says. That Donald with his slimy, cold ways and his shiny glasses so that you can't see his eyes. He's a bad one."

"So he is, Emma," Channing groaned. "So he is and I'm glad you're going to leave, but I want to go too. If you'll help me to get out of this chair we'll go together. You'll want a knife to cut these ropes. Put the candle on the floor and see how they've tied me up. How did you know I was here?"

She did as she was told.

"I knew they'd taken you down here after that row upstairs. How do you know this man Donald, sir? You could have knocked me down soon as kiss your hand when I saw you with him up there at tea-time. You seemed all friendly one minute and the next thing I know is they're carrying you down these stairs and then taking the old chair out of the kitchen."

"Yes, Emma, I understand all that. I don't like Mr Donald any more than you do and I've got to get out of here as quickly as I can. Go and get a knife and cut me free, if you please."

She lifted the candle again and looked at him carefully.

"They've hit you about bad, Mr Channing. This lot's up to no good. I've found out a thing or two I can tell you. And there's that red-headed Molly too. She's a bad girl I'll be bound, and——"

"I know, Emma. I know. *Are you going to help me to get out of here or not?* If you don't cut these ropes soon I shan't be able to stand."

"That's what I came for, isn't it?" she muttered sulkily. "Easy enough for me to clear out by myself. I've got my bag packed ready in the kitchen, and they're all asleep upstairs, I hope. I knew they'd got you down here and when I took him in a drink just afore he went up to bed I saw him put a big key in a drawer of his desk. So why are you asking if I'm going to help you? That's why I'm here. I hope you're all right Mr Channing. You seem a bit queer to me."

By now Channing really did feel queer. He was cold, hungry, and in considerable pain, and this ridiculous woman seemed to be as stupid as she was talkative. He was almost too tired now to care but he made one more effort.

"Listen, Emma. If you'll cut these ropes and set me free we can be out of the house in ten minutes, and if there's a dinghy at the ferry I'll row you over. Now will you go and get a knife?"

At this plea Emma quickly unlocked the door and went out.

Only the ceaseless roar of the wind and the rattle of some window shutter outside broke the silence and all he could do now was to wait in patience.

After what seemed an interminable time the door opened quietly and Emma came back. In the dim light it looked as if she was carrying a basket.

"I'd like to be going now," she whispered. "All's quiet upstairs but I don't trust 'em."

"Emma," he pleaded. "Have you brought a knife? *Please* will you cut these ropes?"

"O' course I will. And I've brought you a bottle of milk and some bread and cheese because you look real bad."

She put the basket on the dirty floor and from it produced a carving knife. Next she kneeled beside him and muttering and grumbling, she first cut the rope binding his ankles and then went behind him and freed his wrists so that his numbed arms dropped to his sides. Gradually feeling, and then agonizing pain, came back as the blood began to flow again to hands and feet. He stooped forward and tried to rub his ankles but was too dizzy to reach them, and then Emma rather clumsily put her arm round his shoulders and pushed him back into the chair.

"They've treated you hard, sir. They're a wicked lot, and though I don't know what this Mr Donald is to you, I couldn't stand by and let them lock up a gennulman from Walberswick, could I? Now take it easy for a minute and drink this milk. And then take a bite of food. Get something inside you and you'll soon feel better."

And so he did. He gulped nearly a pint of milk from the bottle and then chewed hungrily at some bread and cheese. His arms and legs were still tingling with pins and needles when he sat up, whispered his thanks to Emma and then tried to stand. This effort was not very successful but she helped him to walk a few steps and he was soon ready to try the stairs.

"Thanks, Emma. What's the best way out? Is the front door locked?"

"Yes, sir. Locked and bolted. Quieter to use the kitchen door. Take it easy up these stairs, Mr Channing. And not a sound. We don't want no trouble from that lot upstairs."

He was struggling for breath when she pushed back the door at the top of the cellar steps and shielded the flickering flame of the candle with her hand. There was now more sensation in his hands and feet and he was feeling stronger. For half a minute they stood in silence, broken only by the roar of the wind and the ticking of a clock in the hall.

He put his mouth close to her ear.

"Show me the kitchen now and put the cellar key back in the drawer of his desk."

She moved quietly and, after gently closing the door at the top of the cellar steps, led him along a stone-paved corridor to the kitchen.

"Now we can talk, sir. You'll be all right here for a bit. We can have some real light now."

He dragged her hand down from the switch.

"You can't do that unless your windows are shuttered. The light could be seen from an upstairs window."

"Let me be, sir. The shutters are up. I always put 'em up in bad weather."

The light went on and they blinked in the sudden glare.

"Sit down again and rest for a minute, sir. I'll be back when I've put the key away," and she went out again.

He sat at the table with his head in his hands trying to think calmly and to make a decision. His duty was to inform the police and to protect his children at the same time, but he would not be able to do either if he did not escape from here quickly. When his captors realized that he had escaped they would probably go to Heron's Lodge, and if his children did not know where he was they would probably be safer. Emma returned. He must decide quickly what to do.

"Now, Emma!" he said, so briskly that she looked surprised at the authority in his voice. "Just listen to me. Put away the basket, the carving knife and the milk bottle where they belong. May as well keep them guessing in the morning. And can you find me some paper? I've got to write a note, and you'll have to deliver it tomorrow."

"Not here, sir. I won't come back here."

"No, not here. In Walberswick, but I'll tell you about it presently when we've got away. But I've got to write it now, in the light. Find me a pencil and paper and then cut me some more food and put it in a bag."

She looked surprised but did as she was told.

The note did not take long to write and after folding it and putting it in an inside pocket he picked up Emma's suitcase.

"Off we go, Emma. If the back door has a key, lock it on the outside and give me the key. Might be useful."

Three minutes later they were in the yard with the kitchen door locked behind them. Channing was thankful to feel the wind in his face and to know that he was free.

It was not quite dark for there was a gleam of moonlight behind the scudding clouds. As they stepped out together on the road they could just see the darker line of the great shingle bank beyond Ferry Road and hear the raging of the sea breaking on the beach over half a mile away. And all the while the wind, roaring in from the north-west, was cold on their faces as they trudged forward.

Channing could not hurry and found Emma's suitcase surprisingly heavy.

"I've forgotten the tides, Emma. Should be right up about now, shouldn't it? Do you know the time?"

"Heard it strike two when I put the key in the desk, sir. Tide's about full now and this wind is going to bring real trouble. Tomorrow is the danger, I reckon. Highest tides of the year, but you know all about that, sir."

Channing did indeed know all about the danger of the high tides at the times of the spring and autumn equinox on this coast. He knew too that a north-wester was the one wind to fear at these times and this brute had been blowing a gale for over two days and nights.

"You don't think he'll come after me in the morning, do you, sir? That Donald I mean. You'll help me if he does won't you, sir? I've got a right to leave when I want, haven't I? Nobody can keep me in a place I don't like, can they?"

"If it hadn't been for you, Emma, somebody would have kept me in a place I didn't like, and I'm grateful as I'll show you when we're safe over the river. No, I don't think any of that lot will come after you, but they'll want to find me in a hurry. You do as I say and you'll be all right. I've got a lot of questions to ask you."

"I don't like lots of questions," Emma grumbled but before he could speak, there came a thunderous crash from the beach followed by the roar and rattle of the shingle as the waves dragged back the stones. Channing stopped in surprise for this tide must be remarkably high. Then, taking a fresh grip on the handle of the old suitcase he strode forward wondering whether they would find a boat moored at the landing stage.

12. The Message

At heron's lodge, Rose was the first to wake next morning, and as memories of the most miserable night of her life came rushing back she sat up in bed and ran her fingers through her hair.

How wonderful it would be, she thought, if I could wake up one day and know that there was nothing else for us to worry about.

For a few moments she sat still, reluctant to wake Mary who had proved to be such a good friend to her. She thought of the misery and confusion following their discovery of Wilson telephoning to Scotland Yard and of how Paul had backed her furious accusation of Wilson. She remembered how the reporter, after Paul had torn the telephone from the wall, had appealed to David and how, before leaving the room, he had touched her with unexpected compassion.

They had all stayed together without speaking in that room until they heard the front door slam and the sound of Wilson's car starting. After that there was nothing much that they could do. Paul, for once, had made a fuss of her and although David had not said much, he was obviously upset by what Wilson had done. "Better get back to bed and sleep, if we can," he had suggested. "I'm wondering now whether Scotland Yard will telephone the police up here and send somebody round to see what is happening? They might. Anyway nothing will seem quite as bad in the morning. The more we talk about it now the worse it will be."

And because she felt better this morning Rose determined to be more cheerful and to start the day well. She slipped out of bed and into her dressing-gown and slippers and tip-toed to the door. Mary did not even stir. Macbeth raised his head, cocked his ears, moved his tail gently in greeting and then settled down again. His night had also been disturbed!

Rose ran down to the hall, noticing that the time was a few minutes to seven. It would be a splendid surprise if she made some tea and took it upstairs to them all. But before she did this she opened the front door to see what it was like outside. The sky was dull but the wind still strong enough to tear the leaves from the trees before their time, and as she stood on the threshold a flurry of still green leaves from the big lilac in the garden scurried across the veranda and tickled her bare ankles.

On the way back to the kitchen, she looked in the sitting-room. It was in its usual disorder, and the telephone with its broken cords reminded her again of what had actually happened only a few hours ago and which she wished had been another nightmare. She closed the door thoughtfully and went in to make the tea.

Ten minutes later she put down the heavy tray on the landing outside the boys' room because she had one more thing to do before she woke the others.

She was stepping quietly towards her father's door, trying to forget the nightmare of the long corridor, when she saw Paul, in his pyjamas, watching her from half-way down the stairs leading to the top floor.

He put his finger to his lips and came quietly down to her.

"What are you up to, Rose? Did you go to sleep quickly? I did," and then unexpectedly he put his fingers under her chin, lifted her face and looked down at her. "All right this morning?"

She gulped and nodded as her eyes filled with tears.

"Yes, Paul. We soon went to sleep and now I've made tea for all. I was just going to look in Dad's room again without telling the others."

"So was I," he smiled. "I'm sure he hasn't come back, but we'll look together."

He opened the door, but the room was empty. "Don't let the others see how worried we are, Rosie," he said. "We'll get through all this together. I'm sure we will, and I've got a hunch that something is going to happen today. Now where's that tea."

Paul was right. Something did happen and much more quickly than either of them had dared to hope.

*　　*　　*

It was during breakfast that there came a thunderous knocking on the front door.

"I'll go," Dickie said. "It may be Scotland Yard."

It was William Miller. He was wearing long rubber boots over his trousers, a blue jersey and cloth cap and carrying a roll of paper that looked like a poster.

"'Mornin' young fella. I want Paul if you please. Quick!"

Paul came into the hall at a shout from Dickie.

"Hello, William. What's happened?"

"We'd better talk private, Paul. What I've got to say is for you and nobody else. How's Rose?"

"O.K., thanks. Come on then," and he led William into the sitting-room and closed the door behind them. Dickie looked at it longingly. He was not the sort to listen at keyholes but he was tempted. Reluctantly he went back to the kitchen. Paul, looking very worried, came back a few minutes later. He was carrying the rolled poster.

"Dickie says that was the fisherman—your friend Miller," David said. "Is there any news?"

"Of a sort," Paul replied. "Not too good. Look at this. I've got to put it on our fence."

He unrolled it on one end of the kitchen table, keeping the top corners in place with the marmalade jar and the butter dish. They crowded round and read:

POLICE NOTICE

FLOOD WARNING

Public warning of the danger of serious flooding due to high tides will be given by the police by

LOUDSPEAKER ANNOUNCEMENT, MEGAPHONES, SHORT BLASTS ON POLICE WHISTLES

Residents so warned should go to safety on higher levels and return to their homes when advised by the police that danger has passed.

CHIEF CONSTABLE.
EAST SUFFOLK.

"When is the highest tide, Paul?" Rose asked quietly. "I didn't know it was as bad as that. It's the gale, I s'pose."

Her brother nodded. "That's it! High tide this afternoon is the danger. William is worried stiff, and I may as well tell you everything he said. He asked first of all if we'd got any news of Father and I said we hadn't. I didn't tell him about Wilson last night because I didn't see that it would help. I don't think he noticed the broken telephone. He's particularly worried because he thinks Dad might be in danger if he's at sea, but I told him we're as sure as we can be that he's not. Now William is worried about us, because he says that the warning is out and that later today, with the tide at its highest and the nor'-wester blowing like this there's likely to be real trouble."

"But surely not here in Walberswick?" David said. "It would have to be a typhoon or a tempest to bring the sea up the long beach here and over the shingle bank. And even if it did, there wouldn't be any danger here, would there? We're half a mile from the sea."

"You don't know what it can be like, David," Paul went on. "How could you? You don't live up here where the sea is our enemy. It always has been. It's eating the coast away. William said something else too. If Walberswick is going to be in danger he thinks my father should be here to keep an eye on things and on Heron's Lodge in particular."

"So he will be," Rose said indignantly. "Of course he'll come if he can, but he won't *fuss*. He knows that we're not babies. We can look after ourselves, can't we? And I'll tell you something else. He'd expect us all to try and help other people and p'raps that's what we'd better go and do directly after breakfast."

David looked at her with respect, but before he could say anything there came another knock on the front door.

Paul opened the door to see a woman in a shabby black coat with a head-scarf over her untidy head. He was sure that he had seen her before but he could not remember her name. Her face was pale and streaked with dirt and she was breathless as if she had been running.

"You're Paul Channing. I knows you but you've forgotten me. Lucky you come to the door for I've got something for you. It's something you'll be wanting bad but you're to swear something afore I hand it over. I'll be glad if you'll let me in for what I've got is for you and nobody else, my lad."

He stood aside and closed the door after her. "Who are you? I know you live in Walberswick and that I've seen you before. What do you want and what's all this secret business?"

"Now listen, young man, for I'm in a hurry. If anyone comes around asking if you or anybody in this house has seen Emma Holmes you don't know nothing. You've never seen her, nor heard of her for months, have you now? You might have strangers coming round asking or you might not, but I promised him that I'd give you——"

"My father?" Paul interrupted as he gripped her arm. "Have you got a message from him? Give it to me at once. I remember you now, Mrs Holmes, and there'll be trouble if you don't tell me what you know about my father."

"Don't you talk to me of trouble, young man," she said with surprising dignity. "I have got a message from your father but I can't tell you more than that now. He wrote it out himself and I promised him faithful I'd give it to you and nobody else. You'd better burn it when you've read it. I could be in real trouble if certain folk knew what I'd done and that I've been here. You give me your word just like your father would, that you'll tell no living soul about seeing me. You do that and I'll hand over the note and be off on the first bus to my sister in Ipswich."

"Sorry, Mrs Holmes. Of course I give you my word. Tell me if my father is safe and well and please give me his message."

"It's true I don't know where he is now and you mustn't ask me more. Here's your letter, boy. Forget you've seen me and—and the best o' luck!"

She passed him a folded scrap of paper from her pocket, opened the front door herself and hurried down the path to the gate. But Paul did not see her pause with her hand on the latch and then hide behind the hedge as a car passed. He was already back in the sitting-room by the window reading his father's message. It was written in pencil and the familiar handwriting was very shaky, but this is what he read:

Paul. Emma Holmes will bring you this and as soon as you have read it and remembered what I write, burn it. Come as quickly as you can to the old red mill on the marsh. If for some reason you cannot come yourself, ask Rose, but this is a job for you. Bring the key, some food and a flask of coffee. Don't let anybody except Rose know that you have received this note. Neither of you are to tell your friends if they are still with you and you must not talk to anybody—particularly inquisitive strangers—about me. You know nothing. Strangers interested in any of us are a real danger and

Rose, in particular, must not be left alone at Heron's Lodge. Better bring her with you if your friends have gone or get the Millers to look after her. Trust nobody that you don't know and say nothing about me to those you do. I'll soon be clear of my troubles, Paul, and then I'll explain everything. My love to Rose,

Father.

Paul stared out of the window with the crumpled paper still in his hand. If he was surprised to see Emma Holmes only just hurrying out of the gate he did not show it.

I'll soon be clear of my troubles, Paul. My love to Rose.

Then he looked up and saw his sister standing in the doorway.

"Shut the door," he ordered quietly. "Are the others busy with their breakfast?"

She nodded and after closing the door ran across the room.

"You've got a message from Daddy. I know you have. Show me. *Show me!* Is he all right?"

"He sends his love to you Rose. I suppose he's all right in himself but he seems to be in real trouble. I've got to go to the old mill at once but you must swear not to let the others know. Here you are. You can read it."

She read it carefully and then took the matches from the mantelpiece and burned the scrap of paper in the hearth.

"Yes, he must be worried and unhappy to have written that," she said steadily. "What do you think has happened, Paul? Did Emma say where she'd seen Daddy?"

"No, no! Of course she didn't. The whole crazy business is secret, but I must go now, Rose. You keep the others busy, but I know we can't pack up food and fill flasks without them knowing that something has happened. I mean I can't wait until you take them out. I'd like to tell them but——"

"But you can't *possibly* do that. Daddy asks us not to. And he says he'll soon be out of his troubles, Paul. That's wonderful, isn't it?"

She sat down suddenly. "I feel a bit sick."

He went over and rumpled her hair.

"Don't be silly. It's just the excitement. Somebody said something was going to happen today, didn't they? Who was it?"

"You," she laughed shakily. "Come on, Paul. You've got to hurry, but I do wish that I was coming with you. Give him my love, Paul, and don't forget the key of the mill. It's on the brass tray in the hall."

The others looked up curiously when they came back. Dickie was about to say something cheeky, but thought better of it when he realized how excited Paul and Rose looked.

"Any good news?" David asked.

Paul said, "This sounds awful, I know, but we're not allowed to tell you anything. It's a promise I must keep and I can only ask you to try to understand. I've got to go out as soon as I've packed up some food . . . Make some coffee quickly, Rosie. I can't even tell you where I'm going, but Rose is going to stay with you, and I'm sure you'll all be able to help in the village."

"Don't see why not," David nodded. "Anything else you can tell me, Paul? When are you coming back?"

"I don't know yet. It would be a good idea though, David, if you all four stick together. Don't separate and it's most important Rose shouldn't go off on her own. Lock up the house when you go out together but all go or all stay. Don't answer any questions from any strangers—personal questions I mean about my father or where I've gone."

"That won't be difficult," Dickie said quickly. "We don't know where you've gone."

"You can leave strangers to us, Paul," Mary added. "Let's help you now. What do you want to eat?"

Between them they made some sandwiches. Rose added a hunk of cheese and three bananas and packed all the food, with two flasks of sweet coffee, in an old rucksack and then they all went to the front door with Paul.

The wind was very strong again and as they stood on the veranda they could hear the distant roar of the sea. There were quite a lot of people hurrying up and down the village street now and people rarely hurried in Walberswick.

Paul drew David a few paces away from the others.

"See the flood-warning poster is put up on the fence, please, David. The dangerous tide is this afternoon and if there's trouble in Walberswick you're not to wait for me, but leave a note under the knocker or under the mat to tell me where you've gone. If it's likely to be the biggest tide ever, they'll probably evacuate you all to Blythburgh which is on higher ground. But don't worry about me, I'll be all right, I promise you, and please don't answer any questions from anybody. And that goes specially for James Wilson if he ever has the nerve to turn up again . . . Cheerio!"

"Good luck!" David smiled as if he was in the secret. "I'll look after this lot."

Then Rose ran forward and whispered, "Give Father my love and tell him why I couldn't come. We'll be all right, Paul, but bring him home soon."

Paul was not sure which way to approach the old mill. Although it was unlikely that anybody would be out on the marshes today he did not want to be seen or followed. There was a way inland along a narrow path by the side of a big dyke, but the quicker way—although longer in distance— was that used by Rose on the day he had gone to London. He chose this route along the track under the great bank which stretched from the mouth of the river at Walberswick almost as far as Dunwich in the south.

He climbed the great bank and, at the top, was nearly blown backwards by the wind. He had never known anything like this and for the first time was scared of what might happen. The sky was grey as lead without any clouds. Away on the north-eastern horizon there was an odd sort of cold light above the line of the sea, but it seemed as if there was nothing in the world but roaring wind.

Two hundred yards away the turning tide was a crazy tumult of foam-capped waves the colour of weak coffee and cream. From where he was standing he could taste the salt on his lips and above the beach was a haze of spray and blowing sand.

Paul turned and ran down the steps and along the path
sheltered by the great bank. It seemed likely now that the
next high tide—reckoned to be the highest of the year—
could bring disaster, and yet his father was apparently
hiding, from he knew not what, in the red mill.

He began to run, the rucksack with its awkward flasks of
coffee bumping on his back. Soon he saw on his right the
lonely, crumbling sentinel of the red mill itself. It seemed as
if there must be a way straight across to it from where he
now stood but he knew there was not. Many a time in high
summer, Rose and he had tried to cross the innocent-looking
marsh from here to the ruined mill. They had never suc-
seeded, for bogs, ditches, and deep dykes had barred their
way. From the shore there was only the one route along a
narrow causeway built above a winding dyke. This way was
only possible in daylight. In fog or in the dark, just one false
step would have meant the sinister dark waters of the dyke,
and a slender chance of scrambling out of the black mud
through the reeds which could cut the hands like sharp
knives.

So Paul, desperate now to find his father as soon as
possible, hurried forward again. So certain was he that he
was alone that he did not trouble to look behind him until
he had turned off the path and crossed a wide ditch by a
shaky footbridge on to the causeway.

About three hundred yards away a man was leaning
against the great bank. He seemed to be watching him but
he neither moved nor made any sign. He was too far off for
Paul to see his face against the dark background. It was
absurd, of course, but Paul suddenly had the feeling that
he was being followed. His father had warned him of
strangers who were to be avoided and feared. Why, on this
of all mornings, in this sort of weather, should a man choose
such a place for a solitary walk? Perhaps he was a bird
watcher? Paul strained his eyes in vain to see whether the
stranger was using binoculars. For a crazy moment Paul
wondered whether the mysterious stranger was indeed a
man? It might be a woman in trousers and it might be

Molly who had been so interested in them yesterday.

What was he to do? Stay where he was to see whether the stranger moved first? He knew that he could easily be seen standing on the causeway outlined against the sky. But he could not stay where he was all day when his father was waiting for him, so he moved forward and for a hundred yards resisted the temptation to look back. When he did so the man had disappeared. Paul stood quite still with the wind buffeting him, flattening the bulrushes and whipping the waters of the dyke into sizeable waves. There was no longer a mysterious shadow against the bank, nor was there a man on the little bridge or on the causeway behind him. He might possibly be hiding in the reeds and it occurred to Paul that he too, might do this and set a trap for the stranger.

He dropped to the ground and wriggled off the causeway into some long grass at the edge of the dyke. He lay there, with thumping heart, for five interminable minutes but nobody came along the path. He got up again and went on. He did not look back again until he was within a hundred yards of the deserted mill. This time he was nearly certain— but not positive—that a shadowy figure behind dropped into the grass at the side of the path as he had done. Perhaps his eyes or nerves were playing him tricks! Nothing moved now. Not even a bird.

Now what to do? Should he walk back to see if he could find anybody? Suppose he did? How much better off would he be and how could he deal with the situation? And if he was imagining things and nobody was there he would just be wasting time! Suddenly he made up his mind, remembering that from the top of the mill it was possible to see for at least a mile across the marsh. If he was being followed, surely the best way to find out was from the mill itself, but it would be silly to be seen walking straight up to it. So he slipped down below the level of the causeway again and crawled, with the rucksack awkward and painful on his back, towards the mill. This journey took ten uncomfortable minutes, but at last he tumbled into the overgrown, dry ditch round the old brick building knowing that at last he was out of sight of anybody on the causeway.

He sat up and struggled out of the straps of the rucksack and then heard his father's voice.

"Good chap, Paul. Unlock the padlock and get inside as quickly as you can. I've got to stay hidden for a few hours. Hope you've brought a hot drink."

He must have been hiding on the other side of the mill but, for a moment, Paul was so shocked by the sight of him that he could not speak. One knee of his trousers was torn, his hair was unkempt and wild, he was unshaven and his face was cruelly bruised.

"Hello, Father," he said at last. "You don't look too good, but here's the key so you can unlock quickly and we'll get inside. I'm not sure but I believe I've been followed here. I had to risk being followed to warn you."

"*Warn* me, Paul? What about? What's happened?"

"Maybe I could tell you," said James Wilson, who was standing a few feet away on the path smiling at them.

"Sorry to be so dramatic, Paul," he went on, "but I thought there was a chance that you might lead me to your father. How do you do, Mr Channing. I want to see you badly. I've already met your son and I suggest we get inside this place and talk. I've an idea that a lot of things are going to happen today and we've no time to waste!"

13. Crisis

As the tattered flags of dawn streaked the eastern sky on the morning of the events described in the last chapter, the coast-guard, in his look-out on Gun Hill, Southwold, searched the horizon with his binoculars.

It was still too dark to see the waves but he knew, and had reported by telephone, that the tide which was now ebbing had been the highest and most dangerous he had ever seen on this coast.

It was a wicked, sullen sea—the most frightening that the coast-guard had ever seen. He swung his binoculars towards the south where it was now light enough for him to see the gentle sweep of Sole Bay past Walberswick to Dunwich. He could see clearly now where the river Blyth ran out to sea and the white line of breakers along the sandy beach by Walberswick marshes. He wondered how much more of the cliffs of Dunwich would be washed away during the next twenty-four hours, and what treasures of that ancient port would be found on the beach after the gale was over.

It was light now, and as the lighthouse gave its last warning until dusk the coast-guard put down the binoculars, lifted the telephone receiver and gave his report. Although he would soon be going off duty, he did not expect to have much sleep during the next twelve hours.

As the tide went down and another day began, the alert was sounded first in the northern ports. Through the River Boards who are responsible for the rivers, where they flood and how they drain the land through which they run, the warning went to the police. And so in the County Headquarters of Police and in every police station, quick action was taken. While patrol cars were called to warn people living in low-lying areas, and policemen in vulnerable villages took out posters like that brought by William Miller to Heron's Lodge, further warnings were sent out. First to the Town Halls and Council Offices of all the towns in danger where the officer in charge alerted the Gas and Electricity undertakings, the Fire, Ambulance and Water Services, the Hospitals and First-Aid organizations, as well as their own workmen and transport contractors.

The Women's Voluntary Service, which have so often done such wonderful work in an emergency, were also warned by the police and their efficient corps of volunteers went into action. Halls in inland towns and in villages on higher ground were prepared to shelter those who might lose their homes. Blankets, dry clothing for children, gigantic urns for tea-making, were all collected and taken to where they would be most needed.

And so, while the different people in our story started their day of crisis in various ways as we shall see, the warning went out and action was taken from the Wash to the Thames. Farmers began to move their stock from low-lying pastures near the sea, fishermen up and down the coast and in the estuaries moved their boats from the beaches, and on the promenades of Southwold and Aldeburgh men worked frantically to dismantle and remove the beach-huts. As the fateful hours passed the wind dropped, but the wise ones shook their heads and said that it would blow a gale again as soon as the tide turned. They were right.

None of those sleeping at Yoxleys woke early on this fateful morning. Donald had told Emma to call him at eight o'clock with tea, and Molly had persuaded the housekeeper to do the same for her at nine if she had not been sent for earlier. Brown and Smith, sharing an attic room, were not interested in morning tea, nor were they very interested in each other.

Donald had a lot to think about and did not have a good night. The booming of the wind and the creaking floorboards of the old house irritated him and he tossed and turned fitfully until nearly three o'clock. Emma never knew that he was awake when she tiptoed with her suitcase past his closed door on her way to rescue Channing. For a few hours he slept heavily, and then woke suddenly at twenty past eight with the feeling that something was wrong. He called, "Come in," thinking that Emma's knock had wakened him, but there was no response and no tea-tray on his bedside table. He got out of bed in a rage and went downstairs to the kitchen.

There was nobody there, nor was there a tray of tea on the table. He listened at the top of the cellar steps, but no sound save the ticking of the clock broke the silence. Donald was sure that by now his prisoner would be very uncomfortable, but perhaps so exhausted that he was unconscious or asleep. He had no time to spare for Channing yet, and indeed had not made up his mind what to do with him, realizing only now that he had not handled this situation very skilfully.

He went back to the kitchen, filled the electric kettle and plugged it in. Then he stormed upstairs to the top landing and banged on Emma's door. There was no reply. He banged again and shouted. Silence but for a prolonged trumpeting snore from the room shared by the two men, so he crossed the landing and opened that door.

Smith woke first with a muttered curse. Brown, an enormous and menacing bulk under the bedclothes, just snored.

"What's wrong, guv'nor?" Smith sneezed violently and then asked, "Who's making all that row?"

"I am," Donald said. "Do you mind if I make a noise in my own house? Thank you *very* much. Perhaps you will both be kind enough to rouse yourselves and come downstairs. You may have forgotten that we have a prisoner. I'm sure that I can rely upon you to wake your charming colleague . . . *Get up! And hurry.* Emma has overslept."

He slammed the door behind him and then banged again on the housekeeper's.

"If you don't answer I shall come in!" he shouted.

There was no reply so he opened the door and saw that Emma had gone. The bed was made so he did not know for

certain whether she had slept in it. The little room was tidy
—too tidy. No clothes and no possessions. No note addressed
to him. Nothing at all to remind him of Emma Holmes.

Where had she gone? Home? But he could not remember
whether she lived in Southwold or Walberswick. She had
answered his advertisement in a local paper, and as she was
the only woman to apply he had engaged her to start work
at once. Had she gone to the police? Why should she? A
stupid, talkative woman who never seemed to know what
was happening around her which was one of his reasons for
employing her. She could not possibly know that he was
dealing with stolen pictures, so why should he fear her now?
Channing, of course! She had seen Channing and presumably recognized him. Had she known that he was in the
cellar and helped him to escape? But nobody could get out
of that cellar if the door was locked.

"Get downstairs quickly with me!" he shouted to the two
men in the room across the landing. "Emma has gone off
and I'd like to know what's happening to Channing. Come
down with me and be prepared for trouble."

There was trouble.

Donald was reassured when he found the key to the cellar
still in the drawer of his desk where he had left it, and led
the way down the stone steps with Smith and Brown
grumbling and muttering behind him. Unshaven, pale and
angry, they were not a handsome trio, and they all jumped
and swore when the silence was broken by a piercing
whistle from the kettle.

"You both seem to be rather jumpy," Donald whispered
sarcastically. "Possibly that will wake the girl, unless she's
off too. She will most certainly regret it if she has . . . I am
now going to open the door. Be on your guard. If he has got
out of those ropes he may be waiting for us. Rush him if he's
out of the chair. If he's still in it, make sure that he's not
pretending to be tied up."

Brown was annoyed. "He couldn't get out of them ropes.
He'll be in there O.K., and not feeling too good, I hope."

Donald unlocked the door and pushed it hard back. The

cellar was light enough now for them to see that the chair was empty and that the ropes with which Channing had been bound had been cut again and again and left on the floor. With the door right back against the wall there was nowhere for the prisoner to hide. He too had gone. No doubt with Emma.

The three men looked at each other in a long silence which was broken by a nervous snigger from Smith. Donald was shaking with rage and thinking fast when Brown said, "Somebody must have forgot all about that woman. Have you had her about the place long, guv'nor? And how did she know where you kept the key? I'm just wondering how difficult some of this is going to be for some of us. Bit tricky. That Channing didn't like us much, did he? Do you think he might be somewhere telling tales, guv'nor?"

"I'll tell you what we're going to do," Donald snapped as he led the way up the stairs. "Get dressed both of you and we'll talk at breakfast. I'll decide what we're going to do and I can put my hands on Channing when I want him. He won't dare be a nuisance . . . Where's that girl Molly? Has she gone too?"

"No she has not," came Molly's clear voice from the top of the stairs. "What on earth are you all doing downstairs half-dressed? And didn't any of you notice the kettle whistling itself hoarse? Where's Emma?"

Donald pushed past her rudely.

"And you get dressed too, and be down in ten minutes for your orders. And make the tea and cook some breakfast and make yourself useful. Emma's gone."

Molly gave him an angry look.

"And Channing? Three men to tie him up and lock him in and he's fooled you all. You're a bright lot, I must say."

On this note of bitterness they went upstairs to their rooms. Brown and Smith were down first and made some tea and cut some hunks of bread. They eyed each other furtively and had little to say. Neither really trusted the other, and as they had not yet been paid they wanted their money before anything else was decided.

Donald was next down, looking as well-shaved and groomed as usual. He was calm and looked with distaste at his unshaven, grubby "colleagues".

"While you are my guests," he said quietly, "I shall be glad if you will try to behave in a civilized way. You must be *very* hungry, Brown. I trust that you have left some bread for me and Molly. When she appears, by the way, kindly ask her to bring me some tea, toast, and an orange on a tray to the study."

"Now just look here, guv'nor," Brown said roughly. "That sort of talk isn't good enough. We've got to get out of here quickly and no time to waste. It's no use standing there giving your orders about posh breakfasts on trays. I want the cash that's due to me right now. I never did like that Channing, and I don't reckon he'll waste any time in going to the police——"

"He hasn't," Molly said from the doorway. "There's a police car coming down the road now. I saw it from the landing window."

Donald's voice did not even shake as he gave his orders.

"You two men get down into the cellar, lock yourselves in and keep quiet. I'll manage this if you don't all lose your heads. Molly, into the sitting-room, and remember that you're my daughter. I've been very ill and have taken this house for two months convalescence. Use your wits, Molly. Follow my lead and we'll get by, but we shall be in trouble if they search the house."

Molly nodded and gave him a quick smile of appreciation as there came a thunderous knock on the door. Brown and Smith ran for the cellar steps as Donald picked up the half-eaten slices of bread on the table and tossed them into the pail under the sink. Then with a nod to Molly who went ahead of him into the sitting-room, he closed the door at the head of the cellar steps and walked with dignity to the front door just as the knocking again shattered the silence in the house. He took a deep breath to steady his nerves and then put his fingers on the latch.

A howling gust of wind flung the door back as he looked up at the biggest policeman he had ever seen. Beyond him he saw the police car turning in the yard, proving that there were at least two officers and possibly more.

"Good morning, officer," he shouted above the roar of the wind. "Will you step inside and tell me if there is anything I can do for you? Is there anything wrong?"

"Yes, sir, there is, and I won't come in. How many in this house?"

"Two, officer. My daughter and I. What's wrong?"

"There's an emergency, sir. Every house on low-lying ground in the Southwold-Walberswick areas must be evacuated within two hours. There's a flood warning and the sea may break through. I see you have a car and you've got time to pack up valuables and papers. We shan't be back but unless you hurry you may find Ferry Road closed," and he turned and hurried back to the waiting car.

Donald watched the car drive off, hardly believing in his good luck. Now the way was open for their escape. Nobody would be surprised or ask any questions when they drove off. In the confusion of an evacuation nobody would care or even notice them or know where they had gone. Yoxleys had served its turn and with the stolen J.J. masterpiece safe in his pocket he would soon be in London again and able to make new plans. It might be advisable to go abroad for a while. South America, perhaps. And even if Channing told his story to the police, Donald was sure that he had a very good chance of getting away, although it might be advisable to hide the picture for a while.

All the same, there was no time to waste so he shut the ont door and walked back along the hall. Molly was nding on the threshold of the sitting-room.

"No trouble, Molly. They're not suspicious and I have dealt with the situation. We've been warned to move out quickly and nothing could suit us better. Fetch the others in here if you please and I will give you your orders."

He was standing on the hearthrug when the three came back.

"She says it's all O.K., guv'nor," Brown said at once. "Says the police don't know a thing but we've got to clear out. I want my money now. Right now. So does Smithie, and Molly would be a fool if she doesn't take her whack right away. Let's have the money and we'll know where we are. See what we mean, guv'nor?"

"Indeed I do," Donald said grimly, "but I do not like your manners. Your wages are ready for you," and from the inside pocket of his jacket he took three sealed, bulky envelopes and put them on the mantelpiece. "Molly has told you what has happened and I will now give you your orders. We leave together in the car in half an hour. We shall not be questioned by the police as we have been ordered to leave the district. We drive to Blythburgh on the main London road and there we shall separate. You will realize that it would be foolish to be seen together after we have left here. I will give you further instructions in the car. Leave nothing of value or anything of interest to the police here in the house. Please be packed up and ready as soon as you can."

He passed over the envelopes in silence and then walked out of the room.

Upstairs, he took from under the mattress of his bed the precious J.J. canvas which had been neatly cut from its frame by Brown. He rolled it carefully in a plastic bag and put it in the inside pocket of his jacket. It spoiled the appearance of his suit, but he preferred to carry the picture actually on his person in this way. His bag was already packed, but as he crossed to the dressing-table to check that he had left nothing of importance he glanced out of the window.

His own car, driven by Smith, and with Brown and Molly in the back, was moving out of the yard. He struggled in vain to open the window. He shouted in sudden rage and then, realizing how he had been betrayed, he sat on the unmade bed with his head in his hands.

* * *

The official warning came to Walberswick about half an hour after Paul had gone off by himself to the red mill. Rose was sure that David had guessed that they had heard from her father by the sympathetic smile he had given her when she had said, "Let's all go out together and see what's happening. We may be able to help and I'm too excited to clear up now. What do you think, twins?"

"I never think about washing-up," Mary said. "Twins loathe washing-up much, much more than ordinary people. Let's go out. Mackie needs exercise and although nobody except me ever thinks of it our dog has had a very disturbed night."

David agreed, so they locked up the house and went out into the wind. Rose suggested that they go first to the Millers' cottage and look at the river.

As they hurried through the village they saw that people were taking the preliminary warning seriously, and some were already piling suitcases and belongings into their cars.

Rose led them past the Millers' cottage to the muddy banks of the river by the ferry. The tide was out, and although they could not see the sea from where they were standing they could hear its roar over a quarter of a mile away. As Rose had suspected, there were many more boats than usual moored to the opposite bank.

"There are a lot of cars over by the caravan camp," Dickie said suddenly. "What's happening?"

Rose led them away to the right where they scrambled up to a higher part of the bank. From here they could see the caravan camp and the end of Ferry Road.

"The camp is being evacuated," David said. "Everybody is clearing out. Looks like a police car over there too."

"Yes, it is," Rose agreed. "There won't be many holiday-makers left there now anyway, but they're towing away as many caravans as they can." She looked anxiously at David. "This isn't too good, is it?"

Dickie answered. "You may as well tell us the truth, Rose. We can see that you're excited and worried, too, but do you really mean that they are moving all those caravans and making all that fuss over here because they think that the sea is going to come rushing over the top of the beach this afternoon and drown us all like Noah nearly was if you know what I mean? It couldn't really get over the top, could it, and smash all those houses ker-blimp, ker-blomp? What will happen here? I'd like to see the sea come rushing up the river although we'd be all right here, wouldn't we?"

"No, you wouldn't," Rose explained. "That's just it, Dickie. The sea has broken through once before and when the tide came up, William told me that it came higher than we are now and rushed into the street and over the marshes in the middle of the night. His cottage was flooded."

"Did Paul think it could happen again?" David asked as he turned his back to the wind and looked out over Walberswick. "If he's not back soon we'd better go home and get ready to get out. I suppose they'll make us go anyway."

Before Rose could answer, they heard a booming voice through a loudspeaker and saw a police car pulling up by the Millers' cottage.

". . . Grave danger this afternoon . . . All children, invalids and women not doing official work must leave Walberswick. Transport will be here in two hours . . . One piece of hand luggage only to each person . . . Evacuees will be taken to the Reception Centre at Blythburgh . . . Two hours only . . . Volunteer helpers to report to the *Royal Oak* . . ."

The car turned and went slowly back the way it had come while the speaker repeated his message.

"Come on," David ordered, remembering what Paul had said to him just before he went off. "We'll get back to Heron's Lodge right away and pack up. Whatever happens don't separate. Keep with me, Rose. Come on. Don't let Mackie mess about in the mud, Mary."

"Uttah, uttah BEAST," Mary said as she hauled Macbeth from the investigation of a long-dead seagull on the muddy bank. "You might try and remember what an *awful*

holiday he's had so far. He wishes that he'd never come . . .
Hi! Wait for me!"

They ran back to the road just in time to see William
Miller locking the door of his cottage.

"What are you lot doing down here?" he snapped. "I
warned you once this morning. Where's Paul?"

"He'll be back soon," Rose answered quickly. "We heard
the police and we're going back now to Heron's Lodge to
pack up."

"You'll not only pack up but you must get out of here
with the first lot. We reckon there'll be plenty of buses,
lorries, and private cars to help."

He turned to David. "You're old enough to see that this
isn't a joke. There's a chance that if the wind doesn't drop
the bank will go when the tide comes up this afternoon, and
then we've had it good and proper . . . Those twins and the
dog must go in the first lot. They'll be O.K. My Mary is
helping the W.V.S. so she'll keep an eye on them. Everybody from here is meeting at Blythburgh in a big barn in a
field next the church . . . Now look here, Rose. I'm in a
hurry but there's something I've got to say to you . . .
There's rumours about that your dad has been seen in the
village. We'd be right glad of his help here today. Find him
if you can and let him know how bad we want him. He'll
come if he knows the village is in trouble, but you kids and
the dog are to get out with the first lot. You'll only be a
nuisance to everybody here . . . I'll be seeing you," and he
ran off towards the *Royal Oak*.

"You needn't think that *we're* going off in any bus or
lorry or car to any barn anywhere," Dickie said firmly.
"What did he mean about finding your father at once,
Rose?"

Rose looked at David.

"You guessed didn't you, David? I'll have to tell you all
now anyway. We've had a message from my father. He's
hiding not very far from here but we don't really know why.
Paul has gone to find him and take him some food. He'll
never forgive us if we don't let him know that they want him

here. I'm going to find him and Paul and tell them. I know
where they are and I believe I can be back in an hour.
Please, please wait for *me*, David, even if the twins go first."
And before any of them could answer she was running fast
down the road.

"We're all going mad," Dickie said faintly. "Bats!"

"*And*, if you think we're going to this barn without you or
Rose or Paul," Mary added, "then you're bats too."

*   *   *

Back at Yoxleys, Donald sat for nearly ten minutes on his
bed considering the situation in which he now found
himself. Suddenly he made up his mind. This country
would soon be too dangerous for him and the sooner he was
out of it the better. His passport was in order, and as an
international picture dealer he had money on which he
could live in several European capitals. This storm could
not last for ever, and as he was not far from Harwich the
simplest way might be for him to get over to Holland,
deliver the picture personally to Andrea, and collect the
money. Once that was done, there was plenty of normal
business he could do in Europe. The sea route would
probably be less noticeable because the authorities would
expect somebody of his reputation to fly. But now the thing
to do was to behave as naturally as possible. There would
surely be no difficulty in getting a lift to Blythburgh.

So he searched the house to make sure that nothing of
importance was left behind, and burned in the kitchen stove
the cut pieces of rope from the cellar and carried the old
wicker chair upstairs.

Not until he was satisfied that there was nothing in
Yoxleys suggesting any sort of crime did Donald lock up,
pocket the keys and walk briskly up towards the sea.

Ferry Road was in a state of organized confusion and as
he stood with his hold-all in his hand at the corner he
realized why all this low-lying land was in such danger. A
breach in this bank would obviously mean extensive flooding.

Donald was wondering whether to go up to the nearest

lorry and ask for a lift when a policeman on a motor-bike stopped beside him.

"You're looking lost, sir. You'd better be getting out of this unless you've got a car."

And in that moment Donald had another idea. There were altogether too many people and police about, and although there might be safety in numbers he had a sudden wish to discover what had happened to Channing. Donald still believed that Channing would not want his children to know about the last voyage of *Sea Witch* or of their association. And if Channing was still in Walberswick, it might be possible to persuade him to join him as a partner and to take him to Holland as soon as it was possible to do so. Without the other three and with the sale of the J.J. picture, he could make him a very attractive offer. To go over by *Sea Witch* would be the best of all ways to leave the country for a few months. There was, of course, the risk that Channing had already betrayed him to the police and might already have left Heron's Lodge with his family, but he had to take some chances.

He turned to the policeman.

"Thank you, officer. I have some friends in Walberswick and was wondering whether it is possible to cross the river. I do not wish to add to other people's difficulties here."

"You'll be too late if you don't hurry, sir. There's two chaps with motor boats taking people over, but if the tide comes up fast they won't be able to do many more trips. Walberswick is being evacuated but there's more room to move there . . . Hurry if you're going, sir."

Donald had no difficulty in crossing the river. A cheerful young man in a motor boat took him with two others but told him that the tide would soon be too strong for him to make many more trips.

There were not many people about at the river end of the village, and he noticed that most of the cottages were now deserted with all doors and windows tightly shut. As soon as he had turned into the main street, however, he saw quite a crowd of people round a lorry outside an inn called the

Royal Oak. When he was close enough, Donald saw that old people and children were being helped into the back of the lorry. There was plenty of good-humoured joking and laughter as young twins—a boy and a girl looking alike—helped a very fat old lady up a pair of rather insecure steps held by a pleasant-looking boy of about sixteen.

"Don't you worry, madam," the boy twin said as he pushed her behind. "We're coming, too. You can't do without us. As soon as they knew there was going to be a flood they sent for us . . . Up you go!"

And up she went! Then the elder boy ordered the twins in and the girl picked up a black Scottie dog and went up the ladder followed by her twin. Donald, although tempted to get a lift, at once realized that if Channing was still in the village he would certainly be helping so he looked round cautiously. The bigger boy caught his eye.

"Looking for anybody, sir? Sure to be somebody here who can help you."

"Thank you, my boy. I want to see a Mr Richard Channing. Can you direct me to Heron's Lodge?"

David, remembering what Rose had told them about her father and his message, and of Wilson's telephone conversation with Scotland Yard, thought quickly. Things like this did happen sometimes. Perhaps the luck was really turning their way at last. He took a chance.

"I know where Mr Channing is, sir. Are you interested in pictures too?"

As he spoke he looked directly into Donald's eyes and saw his face change at the mention of pictures. He grabbed his arm, took his bag and swung it into the lorry and then shouted so that the twins could not possibly mistake his meaning.

"Listen, you two. This gentleman wants Mr Channing and you remember that we heard he was already in Blythburgh. Take him with you and look after him . . . There you are, sir . . . Up you go. These twins will help you to find Mr Channing."

Almost before he realized what had happened, Donald found himself in the lorry.

"'Bye, Mary," David said, and unexpectedly, from the top of the steps put his arm round her neck as if he was going to kiss her. Instead, with his lips to her ear he whispered, "I'm sure he's the picture thief. Watch him, twins. We'll come over to Blythburgh soon as we can. Do your stuff with him. We're trusting you, but take care of yourselves."

Mary hugged him.

"We'll manage, David. Come as soon as you can, though. Up the Lone Piners!"

Then the driver of the lorry sounded his horn and David jumped down and pulled the steps away. The lorry moved off and David, watching Donald, saw his hand go to the inside breast pocket of his jacket as if to make sure that what he was carrying there was still safe.

*   *   *

Meanwhile Rose, running, now stumbling, then walking a few steps, made her way to the old mill. Whatever had happened, she knew that her father would never forgive her if he was not told that the village needed his help. Under the great bank where Paul had run not long ago she hurried, praying that she would soon find her father and brother.

For the first time since William's call at Heron's Lodge this morning she sensed disaster. It had not seemed possible then that their village and their home could really be overwhelmed by the sea, but now, as she ran, the wind which had died down for the last hour or so rose again in its fury, howling over the top of the bank and flattening the rushes in the dykes. Beneath her stumbling feet the ground where the sea asters still bloomed shook as the great wave of the greatest tide within living memory crashed on the beach only two hundred yards away. Never before had she been so terrified of the power and majesty of the sea. The air was thick with salt spray, and when she turned off the path on to the little plank bridge which led to the causeway at the side of the dykes, she was caught by the full force of the wind and blown over. As she rolled down towards the water she clutched at some rushes and then crawled back to safety.

For a moment she lay on the narrow path sobbing with self-pity and pain, and when she looked at her hand blood was streaming from a cut in the soft palm. She found a handkerchief in the pocket of her jeans and after licking the wound bound it up as best she could. It hurt.

Then she got shakily to her feet and it seemed that the mill was farther off than ever. The wind was fighting her now, trying to beat her down, and although she forced herself forward along the familiar causeways, this part of her journey seemed like a nightmare and more than once she wondered whether she had missed her way. She fell and as she lay sobbing with her face in the grass at the side of the track she thought she heard church bells. Then she was sure that she must be dreaming because she heard the thud of running steps and a voice she loved, calling, "Rosie! Rosie love! We're here!"

She sat up and rubbed her eyes as her father came running towards her. Behind him was Paul with a man who looked like David's friend James Wilson who had tried to betray her father to Scotland Yard.

Then her father's arms were round her and he wiped her tears away. When he saw her glaring at Wilson, he said, "Don't worry about Mr Wilson, Rose. We know all about him. Why have you come and why are the church bells ringing?"

She told them.

". . . And William said they want every man and especially you, Daddy. He said they can't do without you, and if the sea does break through there's only David at Heron's Lodge, because the twins would have to go with all the other children to Blythburgh, and so I thought——"

They all made a fuss of her, and because she was tired Paul and Wilson hurried ahead back to the village to see what they could do to help. Channing insisted that they should all go the longer, inland route because of possible danger under the great bank, and followed more slowly with Rose. There were lots of questions she was longing to ask, but she was so happy to be with him that she was content to trudge behind him along the narrow track through the reeds.

"I can't tell you everything now, Rosie, but I'm not going to leave you again. It's all going to be different now."

"That man Wilson spoke to Scotland Yard about you, and said you had something to do with a man who buys and sells pictures. We heard him."

"All right, Rose. Don't worry about that either. I've had a long talk with Wilson and we understand each other. He's not a bad chap, and although it's difficult for you to understand we're all on the same side now."

Then he asked her if any strangers had been asking for him and seemed very relieved when she said "No." She then told him about David and the twins so that by the time they reached Walberswick, where the church bells were still ringing their warning, Channing knew everything that had happened at Heron's Lodge. Almost as soon as they were in the village street they were met by Wilson. Paul and David were in the back of the car, and when the latter had shaken hands with Channing he described Donald and told how he had sent him to Blythburgh in charge of the twins.

"That's Donald all right," Channing agreed. "And he was asking for me, was he?"

Then he described Brown, Smith, and Molly, and although the boys knew the latter only too well, they were certain that none of the three accomplices had been in Walberswick.

"They might have stolen Donald's car and deserted him," Channing said. "That amuses me, but if Donald and those twins are in Blythburgh somebody ought to keep an eye on them. The police know about Donald because I asked Emma to deliver a note to them here in the village. They're too busy to chase picture thieves now though . . . Why don't you take Rose into Blythburgh, Wilson. We'll follow as soon as we can."

Wilson agreed that he was more likely to find his story in Blythburgh but Rose refused to go with him. Nothing would shake her, and as Paul and David would not leave Channing either, having already promised to go down to the river to help haul some boats to safety, Wilson said he would take in anybody else who wanted to go.

"I've just remembered something important," David said. "If the twins stick to Donald as I think they will, he won't have a chance to get rid of the stolen picture. I believe he's got it in the inside pocket of his jacket, so if you tell the police about him warn them about that."

Wilson nodded. Blythburgh was now the place for him and three minutes later he was on his way with two women and a budgerigar in a cage in the back of his car.

When he had gone Paul turned to his father.

"We met William and told him you were on the way. He's gone with some other men to patrol the shingle bank and he said that bulldozers were on the way in case there's trouble. Nearly everybody who has to be evacuated has gone now, but William said will you help some of the chaps down at the river? I said we would and then maybe we can get out to Blythburgh ourselves, after having a look at Heron's Lodge. Rose shouldn't be here anyway."

Three men struggling to pull a heavy motor boat up the slimy bank called for help when they saw them and smiled a welcome when they recognized Channing. They were hauling on a wire cable but were only just strong enough to stop the boat from slipping back into the water which was now racing up the estuary. David slithered down the bank and grasped the hawser a few feet only from the bows and Paul came in behind him. Channing had barely added his weight behind the last man in the line when David, to his horror, saw the wire strands of the hawser slowly parting. He shouted a warning which was echoed by Rose standing at the top of the bank behind them. Suddenly with a "twang" the hawser broke, and as the boat slid down to the water the men fell backwards. Rose, in her excitement, stepped forward, slipped on the mud and rolled down the bank. David in front struggled up and dived in after her as she fell into the water, just as a great brown wave of the biggest tide ever swept up the estuary towards them.

14. The Sole Bay Disaster

THE GREAT GALE which, with the highest tide ever recorded, caused such damage in East Anglia, struck with its greatest force in Sole Bay between Lowestoft and Thorpeness in the late afternoon. Watchers all down the coast agreed that never had they seen so high a tide roar so ferociously and so fast up the flat beaches. No sooner had it turned than it seemed anxious to return hungrily to the attack. Gigantic waves rolled relentlessly over the sands and hurled themselves against the crumbling cliffs which for years had kept back the sea from the coastal plain, tore away flimsy defences and breakwaters and flattened banks of shingle. As the tide came up, so the force of the north-westerly gale increased, and although the horizon was for a time clear-cut, the light began to fade and an unnatural twilight, full of foreboding, closed down on the threatened coast.

Lowestoft was the first to suffer, and although the fishing fleet was safely home the great seas crashed over the harbour walls and through the sheds where the fish were unloaded, packed, and sold. In a few minutes the water was above the level of the swing bridge which carries the main road over the entrance to the docks. Farther south at Pakefield on the outskirts of the town, the curious "double" church on the edge of the cliffs was drenched in spray as the gigantic waves battered at its last defences only a few yards away.

Farther down the coast the damage was much worse, for here the land was flat and there was little or nothing to check the power and majesty of the sea. Two caravan camps were overwhelmed, many caravans were smashed and a man and woman who had refused to take notice of the police warning were drowned when their small car was overturned by the force of the flood.

From all parts of East Anglia help moved into the danger areas. Police in cars and on motor cycles, ambulances, Red Cross and St John volunteers, Fire Services, men from the Eastern Electricity Board, and most particularly the members of the Women's Voluntary Services came to the rescue. The W.V.S. had already opened up rest centres for evacuees in the inland towns, and by now food, hot drinks, and even dry clothing was being rushed to where it was most needed. Repair gangs with lorries and bulldozers were standing by.

From Gun Hill itself, in the afternoon's uncanny twilight, scared observers saw the greatest wave of this great tide roll effortlessly over and through the high bank and sweep across the Ferry Road. They were silent with wonder as the very sea—not a succession of waves—followed the great wave. The protecting bank was swept on to the road and into the little gardens of the houses. Stones, bricks, blocks of smashed concrete were thrown up in a flurry of foam. Some freak of wind and water lifted the roof of one house and tossed it contemptuously into the flood. Front doors so carefully locked but an hour ago burst open under the pressure, windows were smashed and walls collapsed.

As the houses vanished in a mist of spray the waters swept triumphantly across the low-lying pastures between Southwold and the river. They filled the dykes, and carrying before them a mass of rubbish they advanced on Yoxleys, swirled for a few minutes round the garden wall, found the way into the yard and then poured through the unglazed barred window of the cellar.

Then the river flooded as wave after wave forced its way up the estuary and surged over the banks into Walberswick on one side and smashed boats at their moorings against the wooden quay of the harbour on the other. And because the Southwold bank was lower, these flood waters of the river flowed over the track into the pastures and joined those already threatening Yoxleys. Farther and farther up the river the waters rose until the inn a mile inland at Blackshore was flooded and the footbridge threatened.

The next breach was in the bank below which Paul, and then Rose, had run but a few hours earlier to find their father. Here the waters attacked in a different way. As the tide roared up the sandy beach, cracks opened in the bank and water began to trickle across the path and over the mauve sea-asters. It was half an hour after the Ferry Road disaster before it broke right through with a roar of triumph, filled the dykes, overflowed the causeways and surged round the old red mill, and on and on until it lapped the heather-covered hills of Walberswick Common.

By the time the great tide attacked Dunwich the wind began to drop and the strange twilight to lift. Once Dunwich was the greatest port on this coast with many monasteries, churches, and streets. Now it is only a hamlet with the remains of a churchyard at the edge of the cliff and the few inhabitants know all about the dangers of the sea. On this terrible evening they stood on the cliffs which shook under the furious onslaught of the waves and began to crumble as they had been doing through the years.

Down the coast to Aldeburgh, to Orford—where a boat called *Sea Witch* was sunk at her moorings—to Felixstowe, to Harwich, and to the Thames Estuary the storm raged and the flood waters swept inland. But at last the tide turned and the fury abated. As dusk fell, Southwold lighthouse flashed out its accustomed warning and to every town, village, hamlet and isolated cottage within reach of the floods came the helpers to save life, to comfort the afflicted, to shelter the homeless, to restore the services of electricity, gas, telephone, and water that we all take for granted. Bulldozers, cranes, excavators, lorries and gangs of men, forgetting their own weariness, came to seal the breaches made by the sea.

As darkness fell they worked by floodlight, and later by the mocking light of the moon that shone on great wastes of water and a scene of desolation and ruin.

15. Mary goes to Church

THE VILLAGE of Blythburgh is on the main road from
London to Great Yarmouth. It is about four miles from the
coast, midway between Southwold to the north-east and
Walberswick to the south-east. The river Blyth which, as
we know, runs out to sea between these two places, meanders
across Tinkers Marshes and then widens into a great
"broad" which fills as the tide comes up. All this low-lying
land floods easily and is now the desolate haunt of birds.
The river was once navigable all the way from the sea to
Blythburgh, which for a while was almost as important a
port as Dunwich.

On the day of the Sole Bay disaster, Blythburgh became
busier than it had been for four hundred years and this was
the way of it. Because of its position inland between Southwold and Walberswick, parts of which would be evacuated
following a flood warning, and because the ground around
the magnificent church was higher than the surrounding
country, Blythburgh was chosen as the reception area for the
threatened towns and for Walberswick in particular.

As soon as the warning went out in the morning, t
police took charge. So that all traffic for the relief of t
evacuated between the three places should be unhamper
they decided to divert through Halesworth all north-sou
unofficial traffic on the main road.

At each end of the village therefore they made a simp
road block where the drivers of all cars and lorries we
questioned and most turned back. By noon there was
steady stream of traffic from Walberswick and a bus an
two lorries with the first to be evacuated from the Ferr
Road area came from the north. Almost every house and

cottage in Blythburgh was waiting to take in somebody if the need arose, but the main shelters were two enormous barns in a field near the church. In the big vicarage, close to the church, a first-aid post was set up and the vicar was here, there, and everywhere doing all he could to help. In the village street he stopped a police sergeant and told him that the church could be used if necessary.

"We'll light up the stoves, Sergeant. The wind is cold and if it moves round we might have rain. What is the situation on the coast?"

"Not too good, sir. Ferry Road is the danger, but if the river overflows as well at high tide, Walberswick will be in trouble. We're moving everybody from there but people don't like leaving their homes. They don't believe the worst will happen. Thank you for your help, Vicar. We'll remember the church. Might be a good place to shelter the youngsters and the old people," and he saluted and drove off.

Blythburgh was by now so excited at being in the news again that every car, bus, and lorry which arrived and drove up the lane to the church, where there was room to turn round, was received with a cheer of welcome. The lorry in which the twins and Simon Donald travelled was no exception, and Dickie was so thrilled that he waved violently and was nearly thrown over the tailboard as it braked.

"Now what do you think of that, sir?" he said politely to Donald, winking at his twin. "That hasn't taken long, has it? We do hope you are none the worse for your journey. Personally I found it very pleasant but did not expect such a welcome."

Before Donald could answer, a man in a cap grinned up at Dickie.

"You in charge here, mate? Got a ladder in there or have I got to lift you all down?"

Donald, to his obvious annoyance, had to stand on one side until all the women and children were safely out of the lorry, and when at last he was on the ground the twins and Macbeth were waiting for him.

"I told you to go away," he snapped. "I don't want you. Go and play with some other children."

Dickie and Mary looked at each other with horror and then the former said,

"Did you hear him, twin? 'Go away and play,' he said. And that he didn't want us. If we weren't on our very special best manners we would tell him that we didn't want *him* but that we've promised to look after him and help him to find Mr Channing and ——"

"SHUT UP!" Donald roared rudely. "Be quiet and get out," and he strode forward through the crowd and hit Mackie with his bag.

Macbeth had already sensed that this man was an enemy, so without even a snarl he nipped Donald's ankle and dodged when the luggage was dropped with a thud.

Donald swore at the dog before picking up his bag again and limping away.

"Hi!" Dickie shouted. "Wait for us!" They caught him up and walked one on each side of him down the lane from the church to the main road.

Donald soon discovered that the twins were not the sort of children who could be imagined away. Eventually he stopped in the road, put down his bag again because his arm was aching and looked at them as if he had never seen anything or anybody like them before.

"Now listen carefully," he began very quietly and distinctly, although his voice shook. "You have both been very helpful. Thank you very much. Now there is nothing more you can do. I have changed my mind about wanting Mr Channing. I don't want him now. I just want to be left alone, minding my own business. Do you both understand? I want to be alone, and if you don't leave me alone I shall call a policeman and inform him that your dog is dangerous."

A pause, and then Mary laughed a silvery, tinkling laugh.

"You heard that, twin? He said darling Mackie is dangerous. *Dangerous!* He says a helpless, frightened, bewildered little dog is dangerous after he *threw* his luggage at him . . ."

Then Donald's face went very, very red and stayed red for a long time, for wherever he went the twins and Macbeth followed. Sometimes they walked next to him and talked to each other as if he was not there and sometimes they walked a few paces behind. They followed him to the police barrier at the north end of the village and heard him ask if the police had allowed through a big, black car with two men and a girl in it much earlier in the morning. He was told that nobody except evacuees or cars on official business had been allowed through since the block had been set up. The twins listened to this with great interest, and then followed him through the crowds now arriving in a stream of vehicles every few minutes and up to the church again. They followed him into one of the barns and stood by him while he sipped a cup of tea from the W.V.S. canteen.

Then they followed their victim down into the village street again. Sometimes they spoke to him and sometimes they spoke to each other when he could not hear. For instance, Mary said:

"He *was* looking for somebody when we first got here, twin. It might be Mr Channing he wants to see, but it seems now as if he just hates this place and wants to get out. And the police won't let people out of here, will they? I heard them say that they must keep the roads clear."

"David told us that we weren't to leave him, but I'm tired. I wish some of the others would come. Have you noticed, Mary, that he's got something in the inside pocket of his coat? He's fussy about it and keeps on feeling it."

They were thankful when he went up to the canteen again and they could all sit down and enjoy some hot soup and sandwiches. Hundreds of people were now in the great barns but one of the twins was always with him. It seemed to Dickie that Donald was getting very anxious and restless, and he again fidgeted with whatever it was inside his pocket.

Soon he set off once more for the main road with the twins and Macbeth trotting behind him.

The wind was quieter now but the sky very ominous.

Everybody knew that not many miles away the tide had turned and that the crisis would be in about two hours.

Dickie realized that refugees from Walberswick came in from the south and he did wish that David and the others would come soon. They were both very tired, but for the third time they followed Donald down to the police block at the Walberswick end of the main road. They were in time to hear him say,

"Good afternoon, officer. I don't wish to distract you from your duties but shall be glad of your help. I am most anxious to get to Ipswich on urgent business. If you have to turn a car back perhaps you would ask the driver to give me a lift? I had hoped to meet friends here but cannot find them. I see a car approaching now."

The constable nodded.

"That's a police car, sir No reason why you shouldn't go south if there's a chance. We shall have to ask for your name and where you're going. If there's a catastrophe we have to account for everybody. Wait here, if you please, sir. Are you taking these children and the dog with you?"

Donald met the twins' eager, friendly smiles with a fierce grimace and then turned to look at the police car as it pulled up beside them. A man in a soft felt hat and a loose tweed overcoat got out and spoke quietly to the constable.

"How are things going?" they heard him say. "Expecting real trouble, I hear. I'm after something very different but shan't get in your way. Have you seen a reporter from the *Clarion*? Name of Wilson."

The twins were now like two eager little terriers. Not only were they interested to hear Wilson mentioned but, without exchanging a word, they were both sure that they had seen this man, who was obviously a detective, somewhere before. Donald then suddenly turned away and pushed them aside as the detective stepped forward and spoke to him.

"Good afternoon, sir. Surely I'm speaking to Mr Simon Donald? I was hoping to see you."

"No, no!" Donald denied, plucking nervously at the

pocket of his coat. "That's not me. Turner is the name. You've made a mistake. I'll be back presently."

The detective with a puzzled frown looked first at Donald and then at the twins as they turned and followed the picture dealer again. When he was out of sight of the police car, Donald stopped and waited for them. They noticed that he was very agitated and that his hand shook as he took out his notecase.

"I want us to be good friends," he said in a horrid, silky voice. "The best of friends. I was wrong to be rude to you and now I want to give you both a nice present, and to ask you not to bother me any more. And if anybody asks you any questions about me just pretend that you've never seen me. Don't tell anybody anything about me. Now! Here is two pounds each."

He held out the money and looked surprised when both stepped back in disgust. Before they could say anything a man came running up the lane towards the church.

"Water's over the road down there!" he shouted. "You can see it flooding up fast. If it goes on like this now we'll be cut off from the north in an hour."

Donald looked back over his shoulder towards the police car and then followed the stranger up the lane. At the same time the twins heard someone calling their name and saw James Wilson forcing his way towards them through the excited crowd.

"Follow Donald," Dickie hissed at his twin. "James must have a message for us. I'll see him and tell him about Donald and we'll come after you. Take Mackie. He'll protect you."

"All right, Dickie. Don't be long. Make sure that James is on our side. I'm not so sure that he is."

Dickie nodded.

"What do you want?" he said as Wilson came up. "Do you know where David and Rose and Paul are? An' I don't mean to be rude but are you on our side or are you just rushing round for your newspaper and upsetting everybody."

"All those things, I expect, Dickie. I'm on your side all right—the side of the Channings who are being helped by you. Now listen, Richard."

Dickie nodded again. He liked being called Richard.

"O.K., James. I'm listening. I trust you."

"That's fine. That man you were talking to with Mary— I was a long way off but I thought he was somebody I know. His name is Donald. Where has he gone?"

"Up the hill to the church," Dickie said. "He's the picture man I'm sure, and David asked us to look after him till he came, and we have been. He just offered us money to go away . . . Yes, he did. Honest he did. There's another thing. He's just told a detective, who has come from London and who we think we've seen before, that his name is Turner. But I think he's a liar."

"So do I," Wilson agreed. "So do I, Richard. You two are really good. You're right about the detective too. You have met him and his name is Summers. I saw a police car at the side of the road when I drove up but I didn't see him. I must find him right now, Richard. He's the chap we want. Will you run after Mary and Mr Simon Donald and keep an eye on them both. Don't let Donald escape from Walberswick, Richard. He's the chap Bill Summers and I both want so we'll come and find you as soon as we can."

"You can tell Bill that your picture man is carrying something jolly important in the inside pocket of his coat," Dickie said exultantly.

But James Wilson was already on his way back to the south road block to find Summers, so Dickie, weary but feeling very pleased with himself, toiled up the lane towards the church. He was unhappy about leaving Mary with Donald, but shrewdly he guessed that the enemy was on the run and it was not possible for them to get away from the crowds that were gathered round the church, in the churchyard, and in the big field. People were now standing quietly in groups looking towards the sea. It was a strange scene, and Dickie caught something of the tense excitement of those whose homes and nearly all they possessed might be destroyed within the next hour or so. Nothing that men could do could stop the sea and he wondered, with sudden shock, what had happened to David, Paul and Rose and whether they had found Mr Channing and if so why did they not come.

Mary and Donald were leaning against the churchyard wall. Macbeth was lying at their feet. Mary smiled briefly when she saw her twin, but Donald stared at him as if he had never seen him before and Dickie knew that the man had no fight left. Perhaps they had done better than they thought?

"Good afternoon again," Dickie said politely. "Where have you been?"

"We've been to church," Mary said. "Fancy that!"

And then Wilson and Summers picked their way through the groups of waiting people. Wilson smiled at the twins and tried to draw them aside but they heard the detective say,

"You are Simon Donald I am sure, sir. I thought I was not mistaken. Will you kindly come with me to the police car? I have a few private questions to ask you."

Donald looked round carefully. He met Wilson's eyes with hostility, but when he looked at the twins it seemed that he gave them a fleeting but grudging smile of admiration. Then he shrugged his shoulders and turned without a word to Summers, and picked up his hold-all.

"I'll be back," Wilson said as he followed them. "Nice work from you two."

When Dickie glanced at his twin he saw tears on her cheeks. He guessed that she was suddenly sorry for Donald. So was he, in a way.

Then a woman pointed and they saw a white ambulance coming slowly up the hill behind a car.

"There's been an accident," she cried. "The First-Aid Post is at the vicarage."

As the crowd surged forward the twins went too and saw Paul jump out of the car in front of the ambulance and look round anxiously.

"Paul! Paul!" Mary shouted. "Here we are. What's happened? Where's David and Rose?"

With a wave of welcome Paul ran towards them and they saw that his clothes, hair, and face were caked with mud.

"They're all right, twins. They'll be all right."

"Who will be? What's happened?"

"Rose fell in the river and David went in after her and grabbed her as a great wave came up. Then my father dived in and held them somehow against the bank and we got them out with a rope. David saved Rose's life, twins."

Mary held her head high.

"Yes, Paul," she said. "He would. Let's go to them," and then impulsively, "I'm glad you've found your father."

From the back of the ambulance now appeared Richard Channing also covered with mud, with a blanket round his shoulders and with Rose in his arms. Although Rose looked bedraggled and pale and was swathed in blankets, she waved cheerfully when she saw the twins with Paul and shouted something they could not hear. Then came a nurse in uniform and finally David, rather sheepish and extremely dirty, followed the others through the vicarage gate. Somebody, who had heard what Paul had told them, raised a cheer, and then the twins and Macbeth, with Paul in the rear, followed the others into the house.

The big dining-room had been turned into a First-Aid Post and here an enormous fire was burning. Rose, now standing on the hearthrug beside her father, said with chattering teeth, "I was such a fool, twins. Honestly I was. I slipped in the mud and fell in the river and your wonderful David rescued me and then Daddy saved us both!"

Then the nurse bustled in, said something about a doctor and hot baths and Rose was whisked away upstairs, followed soon after by Mr Channing and David.

While they were away, Paul again told the twins and anybody else who would listen, what had happened in Walberswick after the rescue, and how the river had begun to overflow its banks before the ambulance and the last car loads of helpers had been forced to leave. As he sat before the fire warming his hands with a cup of hot tea they realized that he was still very shaken—not only by what had happened but by the realization that there was a chance now that Heron's Lodge might actually be flooded. At this time he did not know that the sea had broken through farther south and that the marshes, even beyond the red mill, were invaded too.

Then Rose, in borrowed clothes, came down and was given hot milk and aspirin and a seat by the fire. Her eyes were bright and her cheeks glowing with excitement.

"They want me to go to bed but I'd rather be with you," she said.

Her father and David were the next to appear and finally James Wilson arrived like a whirlwind.

"Heard the heroes were all here. Haven't got more than a minute because I've got to telephone London but thought you'd like to know about Mr Simon Donald. He's gone off to Ipswich police station with Bill Summers. Who was it said that Donald was carrying something unusual in his inside coat pocket? I suppose you all know now that the police are looking for a stolen J.J. picture? It certainly wasn't in Donald's pocket nor was it in his bag. I'd give a lot to find that picture. Mr Channing, here, knows that Donald is a thief. Wasn't it David who was sure Donald had it in his pocket?"

David agreed. "I think so. All the J.J. pictures are small, aren't they? Small enough to roll up and keep in an inside pocket?"

Wilson looked across at Channing who nodded briefly.

"He had something like that in his pocket all the time he was with us," Dickie said. "He kept on feeling it."

Mary, who had been sitting on the floor by Rose's chair, got up and looked steadily at Mr Channing.

"Would it be a good thing for you and Rose and Paul and for all of us and everybody if that picture was found?" she asked. "Would it?"

"Of course it would, Mary," Wilson said quietly. "What do you know about it?"

"I didn't mean you, James. You only want to know things to put in your newspaper. You tell me, Mr Channing."

He put a hand under her chin and smiled down at her.

"I like you, Mary. It would be a good thing for everybody except Donald. Of course it would. The picture has been stolen. It belongs to somebody else."

"Very well," Mary said. "I think I know where the picture is. You come, Mr Channing, and James, and my twin. We won't be long. We're going to church."

As they walked down the steps of the porch into the church they were all struck by its beauty. It was very big and warm too. Round an enormous iron stove a dozen or so toddlers were sitting on blankets spread on the stone floor listening to a woman reading them a story. Several old ladies were knitting in one of the pews and some schoolchildren were being taken round the big church by the vicar. Above the roar of the wind round the great belfry, they heard his voice as he showed them the broken brickwork of the floor by the font and the remains of an iron staple driven into one of the big stone pillars. He was explaining that Cromwell's soldiers were believed to have stabled their horses in the church during the Civil War and the pounding of their hooves broke up the floor.

Mary stopped a few yards away from the font and signalled to the others to stop.

"Listen now, and I'll tell you what happened," she whispered. "When Dickie had gone to tell James what had happened I followed Donald up the hill. We did not speak. He walked ahead and I was very tired and rather miserable about everything so I walked behind with Mackie. When he got to the churchyard gate there were lots of people and he stopped and looked round. I know it sounds silly but I was sorry for him. He looked as if he did not know what to do or where to go and I pretended not to notice when he went into the church. I waited until he was inside and then I ran after him quickly. There were lots of people here—more than now—and it was a minute or two before I saw him down there by the font. He was pretending to look at it carefully but he had his hand inside his coat fidgeting with something. I hid behind a pillar, and when he thought nobody was looking at him he opened the lid of that big wooden box by the wall and put something in. Unless somebody else has taken it I think you'll find the stolen picture in there . . . That's all. I don't want to see it."

The vicar and his party had moved on now and when Channing and James Wilson hurried down the aisle Mary said, "Come on, twin. Let's go back to the others."

But Dickie held her back until they saw Channing lift the lid of an old oak chest. Wilson rummaged about and then held up a small, rolled canvas in a polythene bag.

The twins saw Channing point to the vicar and obviously insist on telling him of their find and then they ran out again into the open and down to the vicarage. David, Paul, and Rose were still by the fire and there was nobody else there. When Macbeth dashed across the room to them David got up and pushed them both into the big chair in which he had been sitting.

"You've both had enough. Mrs Vicar says we can all sleep here tonight and you two ought to be in bed now. I suppose he hid the picture in the church, Mary, and it's due to you that it's been found?"

"And Dickie. And Mackie. It was just lucky I suppose that Mr Donald came up at Walberswick when we were getting into the lorry."

"I don't think the stolen pictures matter as much as your father, Rose and Paul," Dickie said, "I s'pose he's had some terrific adventures and now that he's come back to you, the three Lone Piners have done their job, haven't they?"

Mary smiled.

"That's what matters, isn't it? Is everything wonderful for you now, Rose?"

"It will be soon," came Channing's voice from the doorway. "I promise it will. There's going to be a lot for us all to do tomorrow, and tonight when the tide is down most of the men are going to help the gangs fill the breaches with sandbags. You had better telephone your parents in London,

David, and tell them that you are all well. They'll be worried when they hear the news of the floods. The three Channings will soon be telling them how much they owe to three Mortons."

Then Rose said,

"Just think of it. Nobody could possibly have guessed what was going to happen to us all today. But we're lucky, aren't we? Daddy is back and whatever happens to Heron's Lodge it can't be as bad as the houses in Ferry Road. Then I've been rescued by David and it's awful that I can't remember more about it. And then we're all friends together and everybody is being kind, and tomorrow the tide won't be as high and people will help each other . . . Where's James Wilson?"

"On his way to a telephone and London by now," her father smiled. "He's given the picture to the police and says he's sending somebody tomorrow to take photographs of you all. You're all famous and he says he's got a wonderful story."

Rose ran to her father and hugged him.

"There'll never be a story in a newspaper as good as our own private story," she said. "Just think of all the wonderful things we've all got to look forward to together."

"Good for you, Rose," Paul agreed.

But the twins were already asleep in their chair.

The story you have just finished is one of the adventures of the members of the Lone Pine Club. Each adventure is complete in itself and there are now twenty of them. The complete list is as follows:

The author hopes that you have enjoyed this story and would like to know what you think of it. You can write to him, and he will answer your letter, which should be addressed to:

Malcolm Saville,
c/o Armada Books,
14 St. James's Place,
London SW1A 1PS.